THE HIDDEN HEART OF RICO ROSSI

BY
KATE HARDY

MILLS & BOON

First published in Great Britain 2012
by Mills & Boon, an imprint of Harlequin (UK) Limited.
Harlequin (UK) Limited, Eton House, 18-24 Paradise Road,
Richmond, Surrey TW9 1SR

© Pamela Brooks 2012

ISBN: 978 0 263 89319 9

Printed and bound in Spain
by Blackprint CPI, Barcelona

He never reacted to anyone like this. Ever.

But there was something about Ella Chandler, and he really had to make an effort to stop himself twining his fingers through hers, bringing her hand up to his mouth and tasting her skin, brushing each knuckle with his lips.

Especially as she looked completely unaffected by their brief contact. No way was he going to make a fool of himself.

'Wow. This is fabulous,' she said when she'd eaten her first bite of bread.

God, her mouth was beautiful. A perfect rosebud. Again, he had to hold himself back from leaning forward and touching his mouth to hers, brushing his lips against hers until they parted.

And it wasn't just sexual attraction. There was more to it than that. Spending time with someone who enjoyed such simple pleasures…it had been way too long since he'd done that, Rico thought. His last few girlfriends had been more interested in the lifestyle he could give them. Tickets to exclusive events, the finest champagne, designer jewellery. Ella seemed very different. He wasn't sure whether she fascinated him or unnerved him. He didn't have a clue what made her tick—or why he was reacting like this. This wasn't suppo

Kate Hardy lives in Norwich, in the east of England, with her husband, two young children, one bouncy spaniel, and too many books to count! When she's not busy writing romance or researching local history she helps out at her children's schools. She also loves cooking—spot the recipes sneaked into her books! (They're also on her website, along with extracts and stories behind the books.) Writing for Mills & Boon has been a dream come true for Kate—something she wanted to do ever since she was twelve. She says it's the best of both worlds, because she gets to learn lots of new things when she's researching the background to a book: add a touch of passion, drama and danger, a new gorgeous hero every time, and it's the perfect job!

Kate's always delighted to hear from readers, so do drop in to her website at www.katehardy.com

Recent titles by the same author:

THE EX WHO HIRED HER
A MOMENT ON THE LIPS

Kate also writes for Mills & Boon® Medical™ Romances. Her titles include:

ITALIAN DOCTOR, NO STRINGS ATTACHED
ST PIRAN'S: THE FIREMAN AND NURSE LOVEDAY
  (St Piran's Hospital)

THE
HIDDEN HEART
OF RICO ROSSI

I dedicate my fiftieth romance to Gerard—
who always believed in me—with all my love.

CHAPTER ONE

'Um, *mi scusi?*' Ella dredged up the little Italian she'd learned from the phrasebook as she stood at the hotel's reception desk. 'I think I have a sightseeing tour booked this morning?'

'*Sì,* Signora Chandler. With me.'

Ella's jaw almost dropped as she turned around to see who'd spoken. This couldn't be her tour guide, surely? The man looked more like a model for a perfume ad. He was tall, with slightly dishevelled dark hair held back from his eyes by a pair of sunglasses, dark eyes with unfairly long lashes, and the most sinful mouth she'd ever seen.

He spoke perfect English, with the slightest, sexiest hint of an accent. And she was going to have to keep her libido on an extremely tight leash. No doubt the man was used to English tourists who were too full of hormones melting at his feet and he knew how to deal with them kindly; all the same, Ella didn't want to make a fool of herself. She'd already done that quite enough, this past year.

'I, um, *buongiorno.*' She held out her hand.

When he took it, it felt as if her temperature had just gone up five degrees.

This was crazy. How could she possibly react like this to a complete stranger—a man she'd only just met and knew nothing about, other than that he was an employee of the hotel where she was staying?

Not that he was wearing a uniform like the other staff. Instead, he wore a crisp white shirt, the neck unbuttoned far enough to show that there was a light sprinkling of hair on his chest and the sleeves rolled up to just below his elbows, teamed with stone-coloured chinos and boat shoes that would be comfortable for a long day's walking tour of the city. Casual, and yet utterly, utterly stylish, as only the Italians could be.

Ella's best friend Julia would immediately dub him 'sex on legs'. And she'd be right on the money. He was *gorgeous*.

'Are you ready, Signora Chandler?' he asked politely.

No, not in a million years. 'Of course,' she fibbed, forcing herself to sound as professional as she would to one of her clients.

'I'm Rico,' he said.

Why did her tongue feel as if someone had glued it to the roof of her mouth? 'Uh—Ella,' she responded, hating the fact that she sounded so pathetic and gauche.

'Ella.' Her name sounded like a caress, the way he said it.

Help. She really needed to remind herself that she was twenty-eight, not seventeen. And she knew only too well that charm like his was all surface and no substance. Been there, done that and worn the T-shirt to shreds.

'Shall we go?'

'Sure.' She gave him her best attempt at a sensible smile.

'So this is your first time in Rome, and you want a tour of the major sights, *sì?*'

'Ancient Rome, the Spanish Steps and the Trevi Fountain,' she confirmed.

'*Bene.* Then we'll start with the Colosseum. Apart from

the fact that it's the nearest site to the hotel, the queues are relatively short at this time of day.'

She followed him out of the hotel and resisted the urge to pinch herself. She, Ella Chandler, was actually in Rome—The Eternal City. The place she'd wanted to visit for years, though they'd never been able to afford a holiday when she was small; by the time she was earning enough to pay her way, her friends had talked her into going somewhere else with them. This time, she was pleasing herself. Visiting the place that had captured her imagination as a child, far more than tales of princesses and castles.

'I've always wanted to come to Rome, ever since I saw a picture of the Colosseum in a book as a little girl,' she said to Rico. 'I mean, I know it's not one of the official Seven Wonders of the World, but to me it was.'

'It's the largest surviving ancient Roman building,' he said. 'It's not quite as well preserved as somewhere else I'll take you to see today, but it's still pretty spectacular.'

He told her about the history of the place as they walked down the street, and Ella found herself relaxing with him. Then, as they reached the bottom of the street, she stopped dead and just stared.

'Wow. I can't believe we were just walking down a modern street with cool shops and houses—and here it is. Right in the middle of things.' The ruin was huge and just...*awesome.* There was no other word for it. Up close, the Colosseum was exactly what she'd always thought it would be like, really living up to her dream.

'That's one of the things about Rome,' he said with a shrug. 'A building might look modern, but beneath it there's likely to be the foundations of something like this.'

Clearly he was used to it; didn't they say that familiarity bred contempt? He didn't seem anywhere near as impressed by it as Ella was. But she was entranced by the sheer majesty of the ruin; and she was glad that Rico was sensitive enough to let her absorb the atmosphere rather than breaking it up with chatter.

She was gorgeous, Rico thought as he looked at Ella. Very much an English rose with that pale skin, golden-brown hair tied back at the nape of her neck, and blue-grey eyes. An old quote floated into Rico's head: *non Angli, sed angeli.* Not English, but angels.

Ella Chandler was as beautiful as any Botticelli angel. Particularly as she didn't seem to be the slightest bit aware of how lovely she was. And she had a natural beauty—not like half the guests in his hotels, who were manicured and spray-tanned and coiffured to within an inch of their lives.

Why was she on her own in Rome? He knew that she was booked into the honeymoon suite, but he also knew that she'd signed in as Ms Chandler rather than Mrs. So had this trip to Rome originally been planned as a honeymoon? Maybe her fiancé had let her down at the last minute, and she'd decided not to waste the booking and had come to Rome on her own. Or was there some other reason?

Rico reminded himself that it was nothing to do with him. He was her tour guide today simply as part of his on-going review of the Rossi hotel chain, checking that they were meeting their customers' needs with every single service they offered. Right now, that meant taking Ella Chandler through the fast-track queue to a place she'd wanted to visit for years and years and years, and making her dreams come alive.

'I never expected to see gladiators and emperors everywhere,' she said, smiling as she saw the characters wandering round.

'It's fun and adds to the atmosphere,' he agreed. 'But

I'd say just enjoy the view, unless you want to pay through the nose for having your photograph taken with them.'

'Oh. So they're not official—not part of the Colosseum itself?' She looked disappointed, and then slightly wary.

'They're freelance. And sometimes they can be a bit pushy. But they won't be pushy with you, because you're with me.' He smiled. 'And I'm happy to take as many photographs for you as you wish. It's all part of the tour service.'

'Thank you.'

Once they were through the entrance and he'd paid for the tickets, Rico took Ella through into the building, showing her where the different classes of people would have sat to enjoy the shows. He took photographs of her with the iconic arches of the Colosseum behind her and a view over the arena and the basement; even though she was wearing sunglasses in the bright Roman sunlight, he could tell that her smile reached her eyes. And her pleasure in the place was infectious. He'd grown used to thinking of it as just one of the buildings near his hotel. But seeing Ella's reaction made him look at the building again. And he could see what she saw: a truly spectacular place, more than just the iconic symbol of the city. This was the epicentre, where emperors had held processions and entertained the entire city. Where ordinary people had seen lions and bears and elephants, creatures they would never see in their daily lives.

On the second floor, he took her through to the temporary exhibition. 'Apart from the written sources we have, the graffiti gives us a pretty good idea of the kind of spectacles people saw here.' He showed her a leaping wolf scratched into the stone, and a gladiator fighting with a net. Ella pushed her sunglasses up to rest on the top of her head so she could take a closer look, and the expression of sheer wonder in her eyes fascinated him. How long had it been since something had enthralled him like that?

Too many years to count…

At thirty, Rico was jaded way beyond his years—and he knew it.

Not that he was going to beat himself up about it. He didn't have time. He had an empire to run.

When they left the Colosseum, Rico took Ella past Constantine's triumphal arch. 'This is my favourite view of the building,' he said, stopping to give her time to turn round and admire it.

'It's spectacular. Everything I thought it would be,' she said softly. 'Thank you so much.'

'Hey, it's my job,' he said. Mainly to remind himself that she was a client, and that made her off limits. And even if she wasn't off limits, she wasn't his type. He always dated tall, slender, sophisticated women who knew the rules and didn't make any emotional demands on him. In return, he gave them the lifestyle they wanted. Temporarily. Nobody had ever tempted him to make it permanent.

He forced his thoughts back to the job in hand. 'Let me show you through the Forum next.'

'Is this the place where Marc Antony did the speech—well, according to Shakespeare?' she asked.

He laughed. 'Yes. Normally you can hear half the tour guides declaiming it.' He pointed to some columns in the distance. 'The spot where he gave the funeral oration is at the New Rostrum—over there by the Temple of Saturn.'

'Is that what you do, as a tour guide? Declaim the speech?'

She had dimples, he noticed. The cutest, cutest dimples.

And it took Rico a real effort to concentrate on her question instead of reaching over to touch her cheek, to find out if her skin was as soft as it looked. What on earth was

wrong with him? He never got distracted like this. *Ever*.
'I can do. Unless you'd rather do it?'

'I know it's a bit touristy, but would you mind if I did?'

'Sure. Do you have a video setting on your camera?
I could film it for the people back home, if you like.'

'That's so nice of you.'

No, he most definitely wasn't *nice*. His last girlfriend
had said he was a machine, totally focused on his work—
because he'd refused to change his rules for her. But he
supposed that Rico the tour guide would be nice, at least
on the surface. 'It's what I'm here for. To make Rome feel
like home for you.'

Ella showed him how the camera worked and her fingers accidentally brushed against his. Awareness flooded
through his whole body and he almost gasped. He couldn't
remember the last time he'd reacted this strongly towards
someone; and it was as much as he could do to concentrate on taking the film while she declaimed the speech.

'You have a very clear voice, and you spoke it well,'
he said when she'd finished and he handed the camera
back to her.

'Thank you.'

She blushed. Very prettily. He couldn't help wondering
what she'd look like, all flushed and drowsy with pleasure.
Pleasure that he'd just made her feel.

Enough. He really shouldn't be thinking about Ella
Chandler in sexual terms. She was a client, for pity's sake.
So what if she was the first woman to intrigue him like this
in more than three years, since he'd taken over as CEO of
Rossi Hotels? He knew how fleeting sexual attraction was.
And he didn't have time to let her distract him.

As they walked back up towards the Via Nova, Ella
looked enchanted by the wisteria that grew along the wires,

the leaves making a kind of canopy and the pale purple blooms hanging down.

'Hand me your camera and smile,' he directed, and took several shots of her with the wisteria framing her.

There was a secluded corner of his roof garden just like this. And he suddenly had the strongest vision of kissing her there under the night sky, her palm cupping his cheek and his hands tangled in her hair, her mouth opening underneath his to let him deepen the kiss...

Help. He needed to get back to a neutral topic. Fast. Something that didn't make him think about sex. This was so inappropriate, it was untrue. Plus it unsettled him that she could have this sort of effect on him. He'd never found it hard to concentrate on work before.

'What do you do at home?' he asked.

'My job, you mean?' She shrugged. 'I'm an accountant.'

'And you enjoy it?'

'It's a safe job.'

He noticed she hadn't said that she enjoyed it. Odd. Why had she gone for a safe job, rather than one that would make her happy?

As an accountant, she probably spent most of her time at her desk. She didn't look the type to hit the gym or go running every morning. He'd already taken her on a longish walk, climbing up stairs and across uneven ground; and, since she wanted to see several other landmarks as well, they still had a fair bit of ground to cover. Exhausting his customers wasn't a good business idea. He'd better schedule in a rest break.

'Time to flop, I think,' he said. 'Let's go and have some lunch.'

He took her to a tiny *osteria* where he knew the food was good, and found them a table in a little courtyard with vines growing across like a canopy to protect diners from the midday sun.

'This is fabulous,' Ella said. 'I can't believe Rome's so green.'

'What were you expecting?'

'I don't know.' She shrugged. 'Something like London, I guess. With a pile of ruins at the edge of the city, not in the centre of things. But this is amazing. It's special. The fountains and the architecture and the ruins and the greenery—it's like seeing all of history mixed together at the same time, yet nothing's out of place.'

That hadn't really occurred to him before, but he realised that she was right. Rome *was* an amazing place. How had he let his home city become just wallpaper?

'And I loved that wisteria in the Forum.'

He knew she'd love the lilacs in the Borghese Park, too. Though it was too far to go there today, and anyway he was showing her just the highlights of the city that she'd asked to see.

A crazy idea bloomed in his head. The more he tried to ignore it, the more insistent it became. Maybe he could spin out this tour guide thing for a little longer. Ella didn't have any trips booked for tomorrow, and he knew she was staying in Rome for three nights. He hadn't taken a day off in months and he had nothing desperately urgent lined up for the rest of the week, so it wouldn't take his PA long to reschedule his diary.

'It didn't say anything in the brochure about lunch being included,' Ella said, looking slightly concerned. 'I take it this is an extra? I'll pay for both of us.'

That was the accountant in her speaking, he guessed. She'd clearly worked out that tour guides didn't exactly earn enormous salaries, and it was kind of her to offer to pay for his lunch. Unexpected, too; he was used to being the provider, and her offer threw him slightly.

And then there was the fact that Rico wasn't usually a tour guide. His income was more than adequate for his lifestyle. The offer had been kind, but no way would he let her pay for lunch. It went too much against the grain. He gave her his sweetest smile to forestall any arguments. 'Absolutely not. It's all part of the tour.' It was a complete fabrication, but maybe it was something he should take into consideration for the future.

The problem was, he hardly ever carried cash. If he took out his credit card, his cover would be blown—because what would a humble tour guide be doing with a platinum credit card? And he was really enjoying being just an ordinary man, instead of having people bowing and scraping to him or demanding things from him. Ella was reacting to him just for himself, instead of what he stood for, and that was so refreshing. He wasn't ready to give that up. Not just yet.

He made a mental note to have a quiet word with the waiter and ensure that he paid at the bar, where she wouldn't be able to see his credit card.

'If you're sure, then thank you very much. Do you recommend anything?' she asked.

'It depends what kind of thing you like.'

Oh, and that had come out so wrong. It sounded sleazy. Like a come-on. His voice practically oozed sex.

Though he had to admit, he wanted things to go further with Ella Chandler. A lot further.

Luckily she didn't seem to notice that she'd put him into such a spin.

'Is there something traditionally Roman on the menu that I could try?' she asked.

He scanned the menu swiftly. '*Cacio e pepe*—it's a

kind of thick spaghetti with a pecorino cheese and black pepper sauce.'

She smiled. 'That sounds lovely. I'd like to try that.'

'I'll join you.' He ordered them a salad as well, and paused. 'Would you like some wine? Red or white?'

'Dry white would be lovely.' She bit her lip. 'I'm afraid I'm not very sophisticated. One glass is enough for me at lunchtime.'

'That's fine by me. And it's nothing to do with sophistication—more to do with common sense. Alcohol's dehydrating, and it's warm today even for Rome,' he said, wanting to put her at her ease and enjoying the grateful smile she gave him.

He ordered two glasses of pinot grigio and a jug of water. When the waiter brought their drinks, he also brought a basket of good Roman bread, flavoured with rosemary. Ella reached for the bread at the same time as Rico did, and her fingers brushed very lightly against his; it made him feel as though he'd been galvanised.

He never reacted to anyone like this. Ever.

But there was something about Ella Chandler, and he really had to make an effort to stop himself twining his fingers through hers, bringing her hand up to his mouth and tasting her skin, brushing each knuckle with his lips.

Especially as she looked completely unaffected by their brief contact. No way was he going to make a fool of himself.

'Wow. This is fabulous,' she said when she'd eaten her first bite of bread.

God, her mouth was beautiful. A perfect rosebud. Again, he had to hold himself back from leaning forward and touching his mouth to hers, brushing his lips against hers until they parted.

And it wasn't just sexual attraction. There was more to

it than that. Spending time with someone who enjoyed such simple pleasures… It had been way too long since he'd done that, Rico thought. His last few girlfriends had been more interested in the lifestyle he could give them. Tickets to exclusive events, the finest champagne, designer jewellery. Ella seemed very different. He wasn't sure whether she fascinated him or unnerved him most. He didn't have a clue what made her tick—or why she was affecting him like this. This wasn't supposed to be happening.

'So have you done this job for very long?' she asked.

'A while,' he said. It depended on what you defined as 'this job'. He'd been running the hotel chain for three years now, but he'd worked in the business during the school holidays ever since he was fourteen, doing every single job in the company—right from cleaning the rooms through to making strategic decisions. Even now he did a stint in every role in the business during the year, to make sure he kept abreast of the issues his staff faced and could see where things could be improved for the customers.

'Do you have family here?' she asked.

'Some.' Again, it depended on how you defined family. His parents lived in Rome, but he wouldn't class either of them as family. Not after his upbringing.

He could see her slight frown at his evasiveness, and added, 'My grandparents live here.' They'd rescued him from the mess of his parents' marriage and kept him safe. They were the only ones in his life who hadn't wanted him for what he could give them. Or maybe even that wasn't strictly true; after all, his grandfather had groomed him to take over the business, knowing that it would be a total disaster in the hands of his only child, Rico's father. In Rico's hands, the business was safe. To the point where he was planning to expand it outside Italy.

Rico managed to keep the conversation light for the rest

of lunch—and he was pleased to notice that Ella ate with enjoyment, rather than picking at her food and being boring about calorie and carb intake.

And then it was time for the next ace up his sleeve. He'd taken her on the route where she would see the back of the Pantheon first, a squat building with moss creeping over the patched brickwork; he could see from her face that she thought the building a little dingy and dowdy, and was expecting to be disappointed.

Until they came into the square and she saw the front, the huge triangle with its inscription commemorating Agrippa and the enormous columns supporting the porch.

'Oh, my God—that's just what I expected a real Roman temple to look like! And those doors are just *huge*,' she said, wide-eyed.

'Allegedly they're the originals, though they've been restored so much that there isn't actually much original material left.'

Inside, Ella looked overawed as she stared up at the dome and the enormous opening in the centre that was the building's only source of light. 'This is stunning. I can't believe this building is nearly two thousand years old, and they built that huge dome without any of the equipment that construction companies take for granted nowadays. I mean, just *how* did they do it?'

That expression of wonder was back on her face. Although Rico had been to the monument countless times, enough to be almost immune to its beauty, seeing it with her was like seeing it with new eyes; he, too, caught the wonder, as if it were the first time he'd ever seen it. And how amazing it was. It made him want to hold her, feel a physical connection between them as well as a mental one.

Though he could see the disappointment on Ella's face when they reached the Spanish Steps and she stared up the white marble steps to the balustrade and the obelisk, framed by the white church at the top.

'Give it a couple of weeks for all the azaleas to come out and it'll look a bit prettier,' he said.

She wrinkled her nose. 'Sorry. I guess I expected the Spanish Steps to be a bit more…well…' Her voice tailed off and she gave an apologetic grimace.

Special, he guessed. 'They're just steps,' he said gently. 'Where tourists sit to take a rest. Though the square at the top by the Trinità is pretty at weekends; it's full of artists sketching.'

She looked up, as if imagining it.

'Come on. You'll love the Trevi. That definitely lives up to its reputation.'

They could hear the water gushing before they even got into the square, and when they managed to skirt the crowds he could see from the look on her face that the fountain was everything she'd expected. 'Wow. It's huge,' she said. 'I can't believe how white it is, and how clear and blue the water is. And look at the way it's carved.' Her eyes glittered with delight. 'The horses—their manes look as if they're real, not stone, and they're billowing in the breeze, and the water sounds like the thundering of their hooves.'

Rico normally thought of the Trevi Fountain simply as a tourist trap; but right then he could see what she saw. And he was surprised by how stunning it was.

The steps leading down to the fountain were thronged with tourists; Rico managed to shepherd Ella to the front, where she could sit on the edge of the fountain and he could take a photograph of her throwing a coin over her shoulder as a promise to herself that she'd come back to Rome.

'Is it supposed to be three coins?' she asked.

He smiled. 'No. If you're thinking of the film, that's referring to three different people throwing a coin in.'

'I thought I read somewhere…' She flapped a dismissive hand. 'Never mind.'

He knew exactly what she meant—he'd read it, too. Throw in one coin to return to Rome, two for a new romance, and three for a marriage. Was that what she was looking for? he wondered. Marriage or romance?

Though it was none of his business. And he definitely wasn't looking for either marriage or romance. No way was he repeating his parents' mistakes. He kept his relationships short and sweet, ending them before they stopped being fun.

'The fountain was built at the end of Agrippa's Acqua Vergine. It's meant to have the sweetest water in Rome—though I wouldn't try drinking it,' he added hastily, 'and people are definitely discouraged from trying to paddle in it.'

'*La Dolce Vita,* right?' She smiled. 'My best friend's an English teacher and a film buff. She told me about it.'

He could just imagine Ella standing under the fountain the way Anita Ekberg had, letting the water pour down on her. Making her T-shirt cling to her body like a second skin. And then he'd have the pleasure of peeling it off later…

Right now, he thought wryly, he could do with some cold water himself. Ella Chandler was making him seriously heated.

Officially, this was the end of what she'd asked to see. He knew he ought to ask her if she wanted him to escort her back to the hotel or put her in a taxi; but he found himself reluctant to let her go. Weirder still, he found himself actually giving into the impulse to keep her with him a little longer. What the hell had happened to his self-control?

'Time for a rest,' he said, and found them a quiet table

at one of the little *caffès* in the nearby streets. When she'd chosen what she wanted from the menu, he ordered her a glass of *spremuta,* freshly squeezed ruby orange juice, and an espresso for himself. He gulped it down in one mouthful, then gave a rueful smile as he caught her raised eyebrows. 'Sorry. It's one of my bad habits.'

There was a tiny glitter of teasing in her eyes when she said, 'Dare I ask what the others are?'

'No.' But the coffee hadn't restored his common sense. The words came out of his mouth before he could stop them. 'Do you have plans for tonight?'

'Why?' She sounded wary.

'I wondered if you might have dinner with me. If you weren't doing anything else?'

She blinked. 'Dinner?'

'Something simple. Traditionally Roman.' Or maybe he could cook for her. He knew the perfect place to set a table. Even the swishest restaurant in Rome didn't have a view as good as where he had in mind.

Dinner.
A date.
Part of Ella was surprised and pleased that such a gorgeous man was asking her out; yet part of her wanted to run as far away as she could. She might be over Michael now, but it didn't mean she wanted to repeat the experience. To get involved with someone, even briefly. To make herself vulnerable.

And yet this was Rome. The Eternal City. How lovely it would be to share her first proper evening in Rome with someone. And Rico was only asking her out to dinner, after all. It wasn't as if there were any future in this.

Would it really be so wrong to say yes, or to enjoy the

attention? A bit of harmless flirtation might give her back some of her confidence in herself after Michael's betrayal.

Though thinking about Michael meant that she needed to ask Rico something. It was going to be embarrassing, but no way was she going to do to someone else what Michael's lover had done to her. 'I'm assuming you don't have a wife or a girlfriend?'

'No. I'm single.'

'Me, too.' Just so it was clear. And she intended to stay that way. She wasn't giving anyone else the chance to let her down, the way all the men in her life so far had let her down. Her father, her fiancé…

She was tempted to make an excuse, however flimsy. Tell him she was tired. That way, she wouldn't risk getting closer to him.

Yet there was something about Rico that drew her. She enjoyed his company. And these three nights in Rome were meant to be fun. Given that neither of them had any ties, then maybe she should take the risk. Say yes.

'OK,' she said finally. 'It'd be nice to have dinner with you.'

'Are you vegetarian, or is there anything you don't like to eat?'

'No. And I don't have any food allergies, either.'

'Good. Then I'll meet you at the hotel,' he said. 'I'll call for you at eight.'

CHAPTER TWO

BACK at the hotel, Rico saw Ella into Reception, and then went through the back into his office. His PA was tidying her desk, clearly just about to leave for the evening. 'Lina, I know it's late and I've given you absolutely no notice, but can you clear my diary for the next three days?' he asked.

'Of course. Is something wrong? Your grandfather's ill?' she asked, looking concerned.

'No, he's fine.'

'Your father?'

No, and Rico certainly wouldn't drop everything to rush to his father's bedside. He was well aware that Lina knew it, too; she'd worked for the Rossi chain for longer than he had, long enough to know exactly why Rico had no time for his parents and never would. 'I'm just taking some time off.'

She blinked. 'Are *you* ill?'

'Very funny.' He glowered at her briefly. 'I'm not that driven.'

'Actually, you are, Rico.' She patted his arm to soften her words. 'Look, nobody's going to be around at this time of the afternoon, so there's no point in making any calls now. I'll deal with it first thing tomorrow and move all your meetings.'

'Thank you. I'll have my mobile with me if you need to get in touch. Text or voicemail, that is,' he added.

'I'm not going to call you. It'll do you good to have a break.' She paused. 'So are you going anywhere special?'

'Maybe.'

She gave him a wry smile. 'I should know better than to ask *you* a personal question.'

He grimaced. 'Sorry. I don't mean to be rude.'

'But everything personal is off limits. I know.' She rolled her eyes. 'Tell me again why I put up with you?'

'Must be my charm,' he teased back. Then he grew serious again. 'Thank you, Lina. I do appreciate you.'

'I know you do, *tesoro*. It's why I put up with all your impossible demands.' But she was smiling. 'Go and have some fun.'

'I will.' His step already felt lighter. Which was crazy. There wasn't any future in this; Ella Chandler was a tourist, only here for a couple of days. But maybe, just maybe, Lina was right. Having a little fun in his life would do him good.

Rico left his office and headed for the butcher's. It had been a long time since he'd last gone shopping, and it felt odd to be so domesticated. He came home via the greengrocer's, the baker's and the deli; then rolled up his sleeves and began preparing dinner, humming to himself as he worked.

What did you wear for dinner in Rome? Ella wondered. She'd expected to find a little *trattoria* somewhere and just watch the crowds as she ate, or maybe study the more detailed guidebook to Rome she'd brought with her. She'd packed a pretty, floaty summer dress at the last minute; hopefully that would be smart enough, especially if she put her hair up. She knew it wouldn't be smart enough if Rico took her somewhere seriously posh; then again, he knew the city better than most, so he was more likely to take her to a small, out-of-the-way place with amazing food and where it didn't really matter what you wore.

At precisely eight o'clock, there was a knock on her door.

She opened it, and he smiled at her. 'Ella, *bellezza*. You look lovely.'

He was wearing a different white shirt, this time teamed with faded jeans; he looked utterly gorgeous and her heart skipped a beat.

Reminding herself that this was just dinner, she asked brightly, 'So where are we going?'

'I thought I'd cook for you.'

She blinked. 'You cook?'

He shrugged. 'It's not that difficult.'

True. Though Michael had never cooked. He'd always left it to her. And she'd been fool enough to let him get away with it.

'You have a very expressive face,' Rico said. 'It looks to me as if you've been dating the wrong kind of man.'

He could say that again. 'Perhaps,' she said. This definitely wasn't the time or the place to moan about her ex. 'But I'm over him.' And she was following the old saying to the letter: the best revenge was living well. Thanks to her lottery win, she was going to follow every single dream she'd ever had. Ones that Michael most definitely wouldn't have shared.

Rico took her to the end of a corridor, then tapped numbers into a small, discreet keypad to open the door. She followed him up the stairs and they ended up in the most enchanting roof garden she'd ever seen. There were tiny fairy lights twined through the greenery, and one corner was draped in wisteria.

'Oh, this is beautiful,' she said in delight.

He looked pleased. 'I'm glad you like it.'

There was a table laid for two in the centre of the garden, with a candle on the table and wine chilling in an ice
bucket. And she had the clearest view of the Colosseum,
with the three lowest tiers lit from the inside and the moon
rising above it. 'This is just amazing. Is this your place?'

Yes. But, if he told her that, then she'd know he'd been
economical with the truth about being a tour guide. And
he liked the fact that she was responding to him as a man,
not as the head of the hotel chain; he still wasn't quite
ready to give that up. 'It's borrowed,' he said. Which was
an equivocation: he was borrowing it from himself.

She looked slightly worried. 'Are you sure the owner
doesn't mind?'

'The owner definitely doesn't mind,' he reassured her.
'Please, take a seat. May I pour you some wine?'

'Thank you.'

He held her chair out for her, then poured them both a
glass of wine. 'I'll just go and get our antipasti.'

He brought out a platter of *bruschetta* to share.

'Wow, this is fabulous,' she said after the first taste.

'Thank you.' He inclined his head, playing it cool, but
inside he was pleased. Particularly as she ate without fuss-
ing about carbs or calories; the last three women he'd dated
had toyed with their food, and it had irritated him hugely.
He loathed pretence.

And the fact that right now he was pretending to be
something he wasn't… He pushed that aside. It was only a
tiny white lie. And it meant he could be himself with her,
instead of the man everyone expected him to be.

She complimented him on the pasta Alfredo he served

for the next course, and on the spring lamb served with rosemary potatoes and garlicky spinach.

'It's very simple Roman food,' he said with a smile.

'And you've taken the time to make it. To spoil me. I appreciate that,' she said.

'I have a confession to make,' he said when he brought dessert through. 'Puddings aren't my strong point. I bought the panna cotta from the local deli.'

'But you've taken the time to present it nicely,' she pointed out.

He raised an eyebrow. 'You're not a hotel inspector in disguise, are you?'

She laughed. 'No. I'm just a boring accountant.'

'You're not boring at all,' he corrected. 'I'm enjoying your company.' He smiled back at her. 'And I know you weren't fishing for a compliment, before you say it.'

'I'm enjoying your company, too,' she said shyly.

'Good. Come and look out over Rome. This place has great views.' He took her hand, drew her to her feet, walked with her to the edge of the terrace.

She leaned both hands on the balustrade to look out over the city; the churches and buildings were all lit up so brightly that every detail was visible. Rico couldn't resist standing behind her and resting his arms on the balustrade on either side of hers, while he pointed out what all the buildings were.

This close, he could smell her perfume; it reminded him of spring violets. And, with her hair up, her nape was bare and way, way too tempting. The spaghetti straps of her dress were no barrier to his lips at all…

With an uncontrollable impulse, he dipped his head so he could kiss the curve of her neck; she shivered and leaned back against him. Her skin was so soft against his mouth, so sweet—and it wasn't enough. He spun her round to face him and brushed his mouth against hers. He could feel her lips parting, inviting him to deepen the kiss; he loved the way she responded to him, her shyness melting beneath his mouth.

He could feel her breasts pressing against him and he slid one hand between their bodies so he could caress her. Through the thin material of her dress and the lace of her bra, her nipple was hardening; he rubbed his thumb against it, and she gave a little gasp of pleasure.

Good. So it was the same for her. This crazy, unexpected surge of desire.

And right now he really needed to see her. To touch her. Skin to skin.

His hand went to the top of the zip at the back of her dress. 'Ella. May I?' he whispered, drawing her back away from the edge so that the greenery gave them privacy again.

She nodded, and he slid the zip down to her waist. He hooked a finger into one spaghetti strap and slid it down, then the other, coaxing the material down to her waist. Her bra was strapless, lacy and very, very pretty; but it was in the way. He needed to see her right now. He unsnapped her bra, let it drop to the floor, then cupped her breasts in both hands. 'You're beautiful,' he said softly. *'Bellezza.'*

She blushed. 'I, um…'

Yeah. He knew. This wasn't the time for words. He kissed her again, hot and urgent; when she tipped her head back, he kissed his way down her throat, then took one nipple into his mouth and sucked. Her hands slid into his hair, urging him on.

Rico's senses were spinning. He was so aware of the softness of her skin, the sweetness of her perfume. When he finally straightened up and looked at her again, desire lanced through him. She looked gorgeously dishevelled, naked to the waist and with wisps of hair escaping from their confines. He wanted to take her hair down properly, see it spread across his pillows.

But the fact he wasn't touching her had clearly broken the connection between them, because she bit her lip. 'Rico. We can't do this.'

Second thoughts? Well, he'd never forced anyone and he wasn't going to start now. 'OK,' he said softly, and touched the backs of his fingers to her cheek briefly to reassure her before he started to restore order to her clothes.

'I mean, not *here*.' She blushed.

His fingers stilled. 'Not here?'

Her blush deepened. 'It's your friend's apartment.'

No, it damned well wasn't, and his bed was only metres away. All he had to do was pick her up and carry her there.

But he'd started the evening letting her think that the place belonged to someone else. Telling her the truth now would make things way too complicated. He was just going to have to roll with the story he'd created. And how he wished now that he'd told her the truth, right from the start.

She cupped his face with one hand. 'But I do have a suite downstairs,' she whispered. 'We could go there.' She paused and swallowed hard. 'If you want to.'

If he wanted to? How could she possibly doubt that he wanted to? Wasn't it obvious how attracted he was to her?

He kissed her. 'Yes, I do. Though only if you're sure.'

'I'm sure.' Her voice was still shy, but definite. 'But shouldn't we, um, clear up here, before…?' She gestured to the table.

So very English. It made him smile. 'It's fine. I'll deal with it later,' he reassured her, and finished restoring order to her clothes before taking her hand. 'Let's go,' he said softly.

They left the terrace and he led her down the corridor

to her room in silence. Her fingers tightened round his; and he knew she was nervous because when they reached her door, she dropped her card key.

He retrieved it for her, opened the door and ushered her inside. He switched on the table lamps so that soft light spilled into the room, turned off the overhead light and pulled the curtains.

When he turned to face her, she was biting her lip, looking nervous.

He took her hand, drew it up to his mouth and touched his lips briefly against her skin. 'Ella, if you've changed your mind, I understand.'

'I'm…' She looked away. 'I don't want to disappoint you.'

'It's fine to say no. I'd never force a woman.'

'I didn't mean that.' She still wasn't looking at him. 'I'm…um…maybe not very good at this sort of thing.'

Her meaning sank in. She thought she'd disappoint him because she was no good at making love? The way she'd responded to him had told him that she wasn't hugely experienced, that she was maybe a little shy. And he had the strongest feeling that someone had damaged her confidence. Who or why, he had no idea—but he could do something to fix this. To show her that it wasn't true. To prove to her that she was a beautiful, desirable woman.

'Ella *bellezza*,' he said softly, 'the first time between us isn't going to be perfect. But that's not a problem. It means we have time to explore each other. Time for me to learn what takes your breath away, and for you to learn what makes my pulse spike.'

This time, she looked at him. 'So it's not a problem?'

He gave her a reassuring smile. 'No pressure, no worries. This is just you and me. And, if you change your mind, all you have to do is tell me to stop.'

'I…' She blew out a breath. 'Sorry. I'm being really wet, here.'

'No. It sounds to me as if someone made you feel bad to make himself feel better. So I'd say it was his problem, not yours.' He sat down on the bed, scooping her onto his lap. She was definitely struggling with doubts, but not doubts about him. Doubts that another man had put into her head.

The only way he could think of to reassure her was to kiss her. Softly. Gently. Coaxing her to respond to him. Stoking up the heat between them, touch by touch.

He slid one spaghetti strap down over her shoulder and kissed her bare skin. She closed her eyes and tipped her head back; he took the hint and kissed a line across her throat, lingering at the point where a pulse was beating hard, then nibbling the curve of her neck.

She gave a murmur of pleasure, arching against him, and made no protest when he unzipped her dress again. He slid the other thin strap down, and let the floaty material fall to her waist.

'Yes,' she whispered as his fingers found the snap of her bra and undid it.

Colour bloomed in her cheeks as he cupped her breasts, teasing her nipples with the pad of his thumbs.

'You like that?' he asked, already knowing the answer but wanting to hear her say it.

'I like it.' Her voice had deepened.

'Good.' He guided her back to her feet, then dropped to his knees in front of her, gently easing her dress down until she stood before him in nothing but a pair of lacy knickers and high-heeled shoes.

'Nice view,' he said softly. 'You're beautiful, Ella *bellezza*.'

She didn't look as if she quite believed him. Well, there was something he could do about that.

'I'm going to enjoy this,' he said. 'Your skin's so soft. And you smell gorgeous.' He traced a circle round her navel with the tip of his tongue. 'You taste good, too.'

He slid one hand between her thighs, cupping her sex through the lace of her knickers. She shivered.

'I want to see you,' he said softly. He wanted to see her abandoned to pleasure, lost to his touch. 'I want to touch you, Ella. Taste you.'

She shivered again. 'Yes.'

It took him half a second to stand up, scoop her up in his arms and settle her against the pillows. He'd meant to loosen her hair, but he couldn't wait for that. All he could think about was making her totally lost to pleasure.

He kissed her, this time more demanding; this time her response was more confident. More abandoned. Just how he wanted her.

It was a moment's work to strip the last tiny bit of lace from her skin. And then he kissed his way down over her abdomen, taking his time until she wriggled beneath him, arching her body and sliding her fingers into his hair to let him know she wanted this just as much as he did.

He could taste just how aroused she was with the first long, slow stroke of his tongue along her sex. Sweet and salt, and most definitely responsive. She whimpered as he teased her clitoris with the tip of his tongue, swirling round and then sucking hard, varying the pace and pressure until finally he felt her go rigid beneath him, and heard her cry out his name as her climax hit her.

Rico shifted up the bed and held her close. 'OK?'

'Very OK. Thank you.' She dragged in a breath. 'Oh, my God. I'm completely naked, and you're still fully clothed.'

'Because I got a bit greedy,' he said with a grin. 'You can always do something about it, if you want to.'

She unbuttoned his shirt; almost shyly, she skated her fingers along his pecs. 'You feel good.'

As she undid the button of his jeans and slid the zip down Rico felt his control begin to shred. Right now he really, really wanted to be inside her. But he needed to take this at her pace, to make sure she was comfortable with him.

And she took her time undressing him, stroking every centimetre of skin she uncovered, moving her fingertips in tiny circles against his skin and arousing him until he was on the verge of losing control. By the time she'd got him naked, he could barely speak, except to croak the words, 'Condom. My wallet. In my jeans.'

She fished his wallet out of his jeans and handed it to him. He retrieved the little foil packet, but his hands were shaking too much to deal with it. She smiled and took it from him, then unwrapped it and slowly, slowly rolled it onto him. Rico was almost whimpering with the need to bury himself inside her; he sat up, pulling her towards him so that she was straddling his lap, and then sighed with pleasure as she eased herself down onto him.

Oh, my God, Ella thought as she straddled him. This was meant to be just a fling. A one-off. But, seeing the pleasure blooming in his face, feeling the softness of his skin against hers and the hardness of his muscles... The sheer intensity of their connection shocked her.

It wasn't supposed to be like this. It was meant to be carefree and fun and mutual pleasure. No emotions. And certainly not this strange feeling that this was meant to be—because she didn't want to get involved again. Didn't want to feel. Didn't want to risk her heart being shattered again.

She pulled herself together. Just.

'Is that good for you?' she asked huskily.

'*Sì.* Yes.' He stroked her face. 'Thanks to you, I can barely think straight in my own language, let alone in English.'

Pleased, she leaned forward to kiss him.

He slid his hands into her hair so he could angle his mouth more closely to hers, kiss her harder. Working purely by touch, he found the pins that bound her hair, removed them and dropped them off the edge of the bed, then sighed with pleasure as her hair fell over her shoulders. '*Bellezza.* I like your hair down. You have glorious hair.' He stole another kiss.

She rocked over him, taking it torturously slow; Rico's control snapped and he wrapped his arms round her so he could push deeper, harder. And finally he felt her body tightening round him, pushing him into his own climax.

Wow. He certainly hadn't expected it to be that intense between them. Not this first time. He couldn't even remember the last time someone had made him feel like this, the last time when sex had felt this special.

Not willing to give up the connection between them just yet, he held her close. But eventually he had to move to deal with the condom. 'Wait for me,' he whispered.

When he came back into the bedroom, she'd slid under the covers. Clearly she'd gone shy on him.

'OK?' he asked softly.

She nodded, but he could see the awkwardness in her face.

He sat down on the edge of the bed. 'Ella. This doesn't mean I'm going to make demands on you. Or that I'm going to just walk away and ignore you, either. It's up to you where you want this to go next.'

She swallowed hard. 'I'm only here for two more nights after this.'

So there was a defined limit. Just how he liked his relationships. They could have some fun and then just walk away. 'Maybe we can see a little more of each other while you're here in Rome.'

'When you're not working, you mean?'

He smiled. 'Actually, I happen to be off duty for the next couple of days.'

She gave him a sceptical look. 'In the middle of tourist season?'

'There isn't a tourist season in Rome any more,' he said. 'Visitors come all year round. So I can take time off whenever I want to.' He paused. 'If you'd like me to show you a bit more of the city, then I'm at your disposal.'

She thought about it, and smiled. 'Thank you. I'd like that.'

'Good.' He leaned over to kiss her, keeping the contact light and non-demanding. 'So, it's a date. Shall I call for you after breakfast? Say, half-past eight?'

'Half-past eight. That'd be good,' she said.

'Bene.' He pulled his clothes on. 'Then I'll see you tomorrow.'

'Hang on. I'll come with you and help clean up.'

He smiled. 'No, it's fine. It won't take me long. And you look warm and sweet and comfortable. Stay where you are.' He kissed her again, this time lingering until his pulse spiked and she looked flushed and incredibly sexy. 'Sweet dreams, *bellezza*.'

Ella curled back under the duvet as Rico left the room. This was the last thing she'd expected to find in Rome. Romance. A fling. And the way Rico had made her feel...

Funny, she couldn't hear Michael's voice in her head

any more. The justifications, the sharp comments about how he'd had to look elsewhere for his pleasure because she didn't have a clue how to please a man. Now she knew it really wasn't true; she'd most definitely pleased Rico tonight. To the point where he'd actually admitted that he couldn't think straight.

So maybe Rico was right and Michael had dumped his own shortcomings on her. It hadn't all been her fault.

And tomorrow—tomorrow was suddenly full of promise.

CHAPTER THREE

At twenty-five minutes past eight, the next morning, Ella was ready to go. As she'd expected, Rico knocked on her door at eight-thirty exactly. He was wearing pale chinos and another crisp white shirt; clearly he wore the same kind of clothes off duty as he did when he was working.

He glanced at her feet and gave an approving nod. 'Good. Flat shoes. They're comfortable to walk in?' he checked.

'Very,' she confirmed.

'Good. Let's go, *bellezza*.'

Ella locked the door behind her and Rico ushered her out of the hotel. She tried not to be disappointed that he hadn't taken her hand. Then again, they needed to be discreet; this was the hotel where he worked, and having a fling with a guest probably wasn't something that the management would approve of.

Did he have flings like this with many guests? She pushed the thought aside. Even if he did, it didn't matter. She wasn't looking for for ever. These few days in Rome were just for her, and she was going to enjoy them. No guilt, no complications—just fun. A few moments out of her real life.

'So where are we going?' she asked.

'To find beautiful views,' he said. 'And something a

little unusual. And, this afternoon, I think we can do something fun.'

She smiled. 'Sounds good to me.'

As they walked down the street towards the Colosseum, Rico's hand brushed against hers. The light contact sent a tingle all the way through her. Another brush, then another, and finally he was holding her hand, his fingers curling round hers. It made her feel like a teenager, which she knew was utterly crazy; and yet she couldn't help smiling. Today was perfect. A cloudless blue sky, the jumble of ancient and modern buildings that was Rome, and an incredibly charming, gorgeous man to keep her company as she strolled through the streets.

A man who'd given her so much pleasure last night. A man who'd made her see stars. And who might just do that again tonight...

They wandered through the streets together, until they came to a stone wall and she looked over it and saw the river. 'Wow. I had no idea the Tiber would be so green.'

'It's fast-moving, too.' He pointed out a line of ducks that were struggling to swim against the current, then finally gave up and went with the flow.

She rested her arms on the stone wall and peered into the distance. 'Is that the Vatican?'

'That's the dome of St Peter's you can see, yes—but, if you want to go there, I'd suggest going very early tomorrow morning,' he said. 'The queues at this time of day will be horrendous.'

'Well, you can hardly go to Rome and not visit the Vatican,' she said, taking a snapshot of the dome framed by the branches of the trees overhanging the wall.

He smiled. 'OK. I'll book us a tour for tomorrow.'

She blinked. 'But you're a tour guide. You'd actually

take a tour with someone else? Or is that like market research for you?'

'We need a licensed Vatican tour guide and I don't have a Vatican pass,' he explained. 'But right now I have lunch in mind.'

They walked hand in hand along the Tiber. Rico stopped by one of the bridges. 'I know I'm not officially a tour guide today, but I'd be failing in my duty if I didn't tell you that this is the oldest bridge in Rome, built nearly two thousand years ago.'

'You mean it's an original Roman bridge?' And yet it looked as firm and strong as if it had been built with the newest technology. 'Wow. It's amazing to think we're walking in the footsteps of people who lived all that time ago.'

'The more things change, the more they stay the same,' he said softly.

Trastevere, on the other side of the river, was incredibly pretty; the houses were painted in a soft wash of terracotta or saffron, vines grew on balconies and terraces, and large pots of shiny-leaved green shrubs graced the doorways. And Ella thoroughly enjoyed their leisurely lunch in the square outside the church of Santa Maria. Sharing a glass of wine with him, seeing the desire glittering in his eyes—brighter than the golden mosaics outside the church that glittered in the sunlight.

Once Rico discovered that she enjoyed looking round the ancient churches, he smiled. 'That's excellent, because I was planning to take you to see something a bit unusual in another church, just across the river.'

'Unusual' hardly did it justice, Ella thought as she looked at the huge stone disc on a plinth in the portico of the church of Santa Maria in Cosmedin. It contained the carved face of a wild man; his mouth was open beneath his moustache, and wild hair and a beard surrounded his face. There was a crack in the stone going right to the edge from his left eye, and another crack running down from his mouth. Ancient and very, very imposing.

'It reminds me a bit of one of the Green Men you'd see in an English church,' she said. 'What is it?'

'The *Bocca della Verità*—the Mouth of Truth,' he translated. 'In medieval times, if you were accused of lying, you put your hand through the hole in the mouth. If you could take your hand back unscathed, you were telling the truth.'

'And if you were lying?'

He shrugged. 'Then the Mouth would eat your hand.'

'Seriously? You mean someone stood behind the stone and actually cut off their hand?' Very rough justice. Though she knew a couple of people who would've fallen seriously foul of the Mouth. Her father. How many lies had he told? To her mother, to his wife, to however many women who had made the same mistake as Ella's mother and fallen in love with a charming, handsome and utterly faithless man.

And her ex. How many times had Michael told her he was studying at the university library, when he'd really been doing something else—or, rather, some*one* else—entirely? Another charming, handsome and utterly faithless man.

Or maybe the fault had been hers. For not learning from her mother's mistakes. For trusting Michael in the first place. Whatever; lying was the one thing Ella really couldn't and wouldn't tolerate. And she'd never let herself get involved with another charming, handsome and utterly faithless man again.

She pushed the thought away. 'Wow. That's really bloodthirsty.'

'I don't think anyone actually chopped off anyone's hand. The fear of what would happen was enough to make people tell the truth,' Rico said. 'The stone's actually a Roman drain cover, and the face is thought to be that of the god Oceanus.'

'It's certainly imposing.' And there was a queue of tourists posing for photographs, holding one hand through the Mouth of Truth.

'It's touristy, yes,' he said, following her gaze, 'but it's a little less common than people doing the "Friends, Romans, countrymen" speech.' He touched her cheek briefly with the backs of his fingers, as if to let her know that he hadn't been criticising her—merely stating a fact. 'Shall I take your picture?'

'Yes, please.' She joined the queue to have her photograph taken with the Mouth, and paid her donation.

'Would you like me to take your picture?' she asked when he'd taken the shot.

'No need. I live here,' he said with a smile.

For a moment, she thought he looked a bit shifty. But that was ridiculous. What possible reason would Rico have to lie to her? No. That was sheer paranoia, brought on by thinking about the men who'd let her down so badly in the past.

He took her for a quick peek at the Circus Maximus, the ancient chariot-racing stadium; then they caught the Metro to the Piazza del Popolo and climbed up the steps to the Borghese Park.

'I can't believe it's so *quiet* here,' she said as they wandered along the path. 'All you can hear is birdsong—no noise from the traffic, no sirens blaring from the police cars or the ambulances.'

'I come here whenever I need some peace,' he said. 'We could walk round, or we could take a *riscio*.'

'What's a *riscio*?'

He gestured to people passing them. 'A pedal cart for four with a sunshade on top. They do two-seaters, as well.'

'A side-by-side tandem, you mean?'

'Something like that.' He smiled. 'We can see a bit more of the park, this way. And it's fun.'

She wasn't so sure about that five minutes later, when they were heading towards a roundabout and, however she turned the wheel of the *riscio*, she couldn't get the pedal cart to change direction. The notice in the middle of the car warned about needing to brake downhill, and the risk of the cart toppling over. Where was the brake? Panic flooded through her.

'The steering's only connected on my side, *bellezza*,' he told her, reaching out to squeeze her hand. 'Turning your wheel won't make any difference.'

Ella was practically hyperventilating. How could he be so calm? 'There's a road train over there and we're going the wrong way round the roundabout!'

'We drive on the right in Italy, so we go round the roundabout the opposite way to how you drive in England,' he reminded her. 'It's fine. We'll give way to the road train. There's nothing to worry about. Just sit back and enjoy it.'

'Enjoy…?' she asked wryly, beginning to wish they'd just walked.

'Ella, trust me.'

Ha. He'd unconsciously zeroed in on the one thing she wasn't sure she'd ever be able to do again. Trust someone.

'I won't let you get hurt,' he said, gently touching her cheek with the backs of his fingers. 'I promise. And I never break my promises.'

She didn't know him well enough to know whether he was spinning her a line. But she'd go with it, for now.

Once they were round the roundabout and she got used

to the way the cart moved, she found that she actually *was* enjoying it. Just as Rico had promised, they could see more of the park this way; and they could stop wherever they liked to take a closer look at a fountain or a sculpture.

By the time their hour was up, Ella was relaxed and had even agreed to swap places with Rico and steer the *riscio* herself.

'Not so bad, was it?' he asked, sliding his arm round her shoulders.

'No, it was fun, once I'd got used to it,' she admitted, putting her arm round his waist.

They walked back past a bunch of teenagers on rollerblades negotiating a line of tiny, tiny cones. Ella was amazed at how they skated in and out without knocking any of them over, their feet crossing each other, and yet they didn't trip or fall.

The fascination must have shown on her face, because Rico said, 'Dare you.'

'Me? But I…' She hadn't been on roller skates for years, let alone rollerblades.

'Dare you,' he repeated.

Well, these few days were all meant to be about having fun. 'You're on.' It was hard enough to skate in a straight line at first, and she knew there was no way she'd be able to negotiate that double slalom of cones. But then the man in charge of the cones took pity on her and gave her a wider-spaced course.

'Wow, I actually did it!' she said at the other end.

'You were magnificent,' Rico said, kissing her.

'And now it's your turn.'

'Mine?' He looked surprised.

'You challenged me. Now prove that *you* can do it.'

The expression in his eyes grew heated. 'What are the stakes?'

She shrugged. 'You tell me.'

He leaned forward and whispered in her ear, 'If I do it without knocking over a cone, you let me do whatever I want to you tonight. If I fail, I'm completely in your hands.'

She shivered with pleasure. 'That sounds good to me.'

He licked his lower lip. 'Right now, I'm not really sure whether it would be more fun to win or to lose.'

'Do it properly,' she told him. 'I don't like lying and game-playing.'

'OK, Ella *bellezza*.' He kissed her swiftly, then put on the rollerblades.

She wasn't surprised that he managed to skate the same course that she did with relative ease. The man in charge of the cones winked at her and set up a more demanding course with a double slalom.

Rico spread his hands, grinned—and then showed off thoroughly. He was as graceful as a ballet dancer as he moved through the slalom course, his body all clean, flowing lines; Ella was aware of how many other women in the gathering crowd were giving him admiring looks.

He almost knocked over the very last cone, which teetered but stayed where it was. He skated round to Ella, then swept into a deep bow before taking her hand, turning it over and kissing the throbbing pulse in her wrist. Desire skittered through her.

'You've done that before, haven't you?' she asked, not wanting him to see how much of an effect he had on her.

'Now and then. Though I'm a bit out of practice.' He took off his skates and handed them back. 'Come on. Let's go and chill out.'

They ended up by the lake, watching the fountain in the middle.

'I can't believe how blue the water is. It's so pretty here,' Ella said. 'What are the trees?'

'Lilacs.'

'They're not like English lilacs. They don't smell the same, either. But they're lovely. This is really special.'

This was where Rico always came to chill out, because it was one of the few places in Rome where you could enjoy nothing but the sound of birdsong; but the park had become almost background scenery to him over the years. The delight in Ella's face as she looked around made him see the place anew. She was right. It *was* special.

They lay in the dappled shade under the lilacs, holding hands and looking up at the sky. He leaned over and stole a kiss. 'So how come you're in Rome on your own?'

She shrugged. 'It was just the way it worked out. Now was the only time I could go, and my best friend's a teacher—she can't take time off in term time.'

'And you have no family who could go with you?'

For a moment, she looked sad. 'No.'

'And your ex?' That was still bugging him. The man who'd made her doubt herself so much. 'Is that why you were booked in the honeymoon suite? And he let you down?'

'No. I planned the trip after we split up.' Her mouth tightened. 'And he's staying *permanently* ex, no matter how many flowers or grovelling letters he sends me.'

Flowers and grovelling letters? 'Maybe he realised he'd made a mistake, breaking up with you,' Rico said.

'Actually, he didn't dump me. I was the one who walked out,' she told him, lifting her chin. 'As for making a mistake…that's a charitable conclusion.'

'One you obviously don't share.'

She gave a huff of mirthless laughter. 'He probably heard on the grapevine that I won the lottery. Not millions and millions, but a decent amount—enough to give me six months' sabbatical from my job.'

Hmm. So was this the reason why she said that money didn't matter? Rico propped himself up on one elbow so he could look at her properly. 'And you're using the money to travel?'

'A little bit. Actually, I only booked the honeymoon suite because it overlooks the Colosseum. I know it's pathetic, but...'

He pressed a finger to her lips. 'No, it's not pathetic at all. If you wanted a room with a specific view, it doesn't matter what the room's called. Only the view counts.' He smiled at her. 'So where else are you planning to visit?'

'Just Rome, for now. It's the one place I've always wanted to see.'

'Is there anywhere else on your travel wish list?'

She shrugged. 'Vienna, but I don't have time right now. When I get back to London, I'm going to be up to my eyes.'

'Back in the job you described to me as "safe"?' He stroked her face. 'Maybe this money's a chance for you to change your life, find a different job—something you really love doing.'

'That's exactly what I'm going to do,' she said. 'This six months' sabbatical—I'm setting up my own business. If I can make a go of it, then I'll resign properly and concentrate on my business. If I fail, then I still have a safe job to go back to.'

She hadn't let her win go to her head. And she was planning to change her career the sensible way, with a back-up plan. As an entrepreneur himself, Rico knew that meant there was a much better chance of her business succeeding. 'So what's your new business going to be?'

'You won't laugh?'

Why on earth would she think he'd laugh at her? He frowned. 'Of course not.'

She took a deep breath. 'I make cakes.'

'Like cupcakes?'

'Yes, but mostly I make celebration cakes—birthday cakes, wedding cakes, that sort of thing. I've done it for years for friends and colleagues.'

He could see in her expression that it was what she loved doing. Which begged another question. 'You didn't think about making that your job when you left school?'

'I did, but accountancy was safe.' She grimaced. 'We struggled a bit with money when I was growing up. So I wanted to have a safe job, one where I knew I wouldn't have to struggle for money all the time—I even trained on the job rather than doing a degree first, so I didn't have a mountain of debt when I finished studying.'

He'd never been short of money, but he could understand where she was coming from. 'But what you really wanted to do was to decorate cakes.'

She nodded. 'I've done some part-time courses. I did a week's intensive course on sugarcraft, the year before last—how to do embroidery and lace-cut work and stencilling.'

He smiled. 'Embroidery? That sounds more like fashion than baking to me.'

'No, it's a special sort of icing.' She sat up and took out her mobile phone. 'Like this one—I made this last month for a friend.' She handed the phone to him.

He studied the photograph of the wedding cake with its delicate lace. 'You made that?'

She nodded shyly.

'Wow. Forgive me for being rude—I'm sure you're very good at your day job—but you're absolutely wasted there with a talent like this.'

She blushed. 'Thank you.'

'So you're going to work from home?'

'Sort of. I've rented a professional kitchen with a small

flat above it. I moved in a couple of weeks before I came to Rome.'

'So when you get back you'll be setting up your kitchen?'

'And making sure I meet all the hygiene standards—I've got a meeting booked in for when I get back. I've done the food safety courses and I've got up-to-date certificates, so it shouldn't be a problem.'

Rico was intrigued. The way she lit up when she spoke about her cakes… 'Do you have photographs of your other cakes?'

'There's a gallery on my website—except I don't have Internet access on my phone when I'm out of England.'

'I do.' He took his phone out of his pocket and flicked into the Internet before handing the phone to her. 'Show me.'

She brought up the page for him, and he looked through it. Her website was nice and clear; it had contact details and an enquiry form as well as giving potential customers an idea of prices, and the gallery of celebration cakes took his breath away.

'These are amazing, Ella. So when did you start making cakes?'

'When I was a teenager. Like I said, money was a bit tight when I was young—I couldn't always afford to buy my friends a birthday present, but I could make them a special birthday cake, something nobody else would give them. My mum was a great cook, and she taught me how to do icing. And I worked in a bakery on Saturday mornings when I was at school; I learned more about different sorts of icing there.'

It sounded as if she'd had it hard, growing up. But he had a feeling that Ella had also had something that money couldn't buy; the look on her face when she talked about her mother told Rico that Ella had been loved for who she was. Something he'd never really experienced. People only wanted him for what he could give them. His mother, for the hold it gave her over his father. His father, for the access to funds for his lifestyle. His grandparents, so he'd be the heir to the business.

What would it be like to be loved just for yourself?

He pushed the thoughts away. 'What does your mum think about your business?'

Ella's eyes grew suspiciously shiny and she blinked. 'I think she would've said I was doing it the right way— following my dream, but having a back-up plan in case it didn't quite work out.' She swallowed hard. 'Mum would've loved Rome. I just wish I'd had this lottery win a year ago.'

'Your mother…she passed away?' he asked as gently as he could.

'Just over a year ago. She had breast cancer. Otherwise she would've come with me and I could have spoiled her— the way she should've been spoiled.'

Given that money had been a struggle when Ella was growing up, and she hadn't mentioned her father at all, Rico guessed that the man had been either feckless or absent. But he wasn't going to push Ella on that, in case she expected him to trade confidences. He didn't want to talk about absent or feckless fathers: his had been both.

But he could appreciate that Ella missed her mother badly: a woman she'd loved dearly and who'd loved her all the way back. 'Ah, *bellezza*.' He put his arms round her and held her close. 'I'm sorry you didn't get to share Rome with your mum. But I'm selfish enough to be glad that I could share it with you.'

'Yeah.' She took a deep breath. 'Sorry. I'm not going to go all maudlin on you. I'm trying to remember Mum

with smiles, not tears. That's how she was. The more rubbish life threw at her, the more she found to smile about.'

A million miles from his own mother—the more gifts
life gave her, the more she found to grouse about, Rico
thought. He stroked Ella's hair. 'I bet your friends loved
their cakes.' He would've been thrilled about someone
giving him a present like that—something that had taken
thought and time and effort, not just a pile of money
thrown at it.

'They did. Do, I should say.' She smiled. 'One of my
friends designed that website for me on the understanding
that I keep her in cupcakes for a month when I get back
from Rome, and I make her a Christmas cake that even
her mother-in-law can't criticise.'

'Yeah. Families can be too critical.'

She raised an eyebrow. 'That sounds like experience
talking.'

'Not everyone has a wonderful family.'

'You're not close to yours?'

That was the understatement of the century. 'No.' And
he didn't want to talk about it. 'But that's fine. I'm happy
in my job.'

'So what's your big dream?' she asked 'To write the
ultimate tour guide?'

'Not exactly.' He didn't actually have a dream. He'd
been going through the motions for the last year, just con-
centrating on making the business be the best it could be
and getting it ready for expansion. London, next; then
Paris.

'OK. Something crazier, then. To be a rock star?' she
suggested. 'Or to design the best Italian sports car in the
world?'

He laughed. 'No. I'm fine with where I am now.' Though
even as he said the words, he knew they weren't strictly

true. There was something missing in his life. Except he had no idea what it was.

And thinking about that made him uncomfortable. He was fine with his world just the way it was. He was in charge of the family business. In charge of his own destiny. What else did he need?

Time to change the subject, he thought. 'Hey. We've been lazing about here for so long, we're going to be able to catch Rome at sunset. Better get your camera out.'

Ella was absolutely enchanted by the sunset. Rico took her back by the Trevi Fountain so she could see it lit up at night, and took more pictures for her.

'Rome's just amazing.' She sighed happily. 'You're so lucky living here.'

'I know.' He slid his arm round her shoulders, enjoying the contact and just strolling through the streets with her. He couldn't remember the last time he'd felt this relaxed. 'Have dinner with me?' he asked. 'I know a little place not far from here where the food's excellent.'

'On condition we go halves.'

He still couldn't quite get his head round that. His last few girlfriends had expected him to pay for absolutely everything—not that he begrudged the money at all, but he'd grown a bit tired of being taken for granted. 'We'll go halves,' he agreed. 'On condition you let me buy you dessert somewhere else.'

She smiled. 'It's a deal.'

They shared a simple meal of bruschetta and a bowl of pasta; although Ella ordered a salad, she didn't pick at it and ignore the rest of her meal. She enjoyed everything. And she was like nobody he'd ever met. Again, he wasn't sure whether that scared him or fascinated him most.

Afterwards, Rico took her to the best *gelateria* in Rome.

'Wow. How do you expect me to choose from all these flavours?' she asked. 'They all look so gorgeous.'

Eventually she picked ginger and cinnamon, and they walked back through the streets, holding hands and eating *gelati*. She sighed with pleasure as they reached the Colosseum. 'I love this building. It's everything I thought it would be.'

'Yeah.' He couldn't resist kissing her. And when he saw her back to her room, he couldn't resist kissing her some more. Kissing turned to touching, and touching ended with him making love to her in the shower.

Afterwards, he tucked her into bed.

'Thank you for today,' she said softly. 'It's been really special.'

She was right. It *had* been special. Which set all his alarm bells ringing; this was meant to be just fun. She was vulnerable; she'd been hurt badly by her ex and had lost her closest family. And he could only be her Mr Right Now. What did he know of families, of love and protection? For both their sakes, he needed to rein back a bit.

It was just as well that tomorrow would be their last full day together. He was dangerously close to actually wanting to get involved with her. Which would be a seriously bad idea.

'My pleasure, *bellezza*,' he said lightly. 'See you in the morning. Sweet dreams.'

CHAPTER FOUR

THE following morning, Rico took Ella to the Vatican on the Metro. As they walked through the museum, Ella was amazed to learn that they were actually walking on original Roman mosaic floors, ones which might once have lain in an emperor's villa; and then on marble floors that had once graced the Colosseum itself. The tapestries and sculptures were beautiful too, but what really stunned her was the Sistine Chapel.

'I didn't think it would be this huge,' she said to Rico. One corner had been left dark, so you could see how much work had gone into the restoration of the chapel and cleaning the paintwork. Ella just stood and gazed at the paintings, loving the depth to the blue sky. And the famous view of God reaching out to Adam with his finger, something she'd seen on postcards and in magazines, was much more awe-inspiring in real life.

'That was really incredible,' she said to Rico as they left the chapel to go to St Peter's. 'I honestly wasn't expecting it to be that special. Thank you so much for bringing me here.'

Outside, there were the two Swiss guards with their saffron-and-purple striped uniforms, and the guide pointed out the building that contained the Pope's apartment and the window where he gave the blessing every Sunday.

The church itself was gorgeous, and Ella lingered by Michelangelo's *Pietà*. 'It's amazing to think that he was only twenty-four when he carved it. Four years younger than I am now.'

'Doing what he loved. Making the most of his gift,' Rico said. 'Which is what you're about to do, too.'

'I hope so. Though sometimes I wake up and wonder just how crazy I am, setting up a new business in the middle of a recession.'

'You already have a customer base, and word of mouth will bring you more. And when you have transferable skills that you can use to keep your cash flow ticking over, if you really need to. No, you're not crazy at all,' Rico said. 'You're doing the right thing. And when you're old, you can look back without regrets or wondering what would've happened if you'd given your dreams a chance.'

'I guess so.'

They wandered back outside into the sunshine, and Rico showed Ella the disappearing columns.

'That's clever.'

'And you're thinking about how you can use that on a cake, aren't you?' he asked, smiling.

'Something like that,' she admitted. She looked at the obelisk in the centre of the square. 'I take it that that's another of the Egyptian obelisks that seem to be everywhere?'

'Yup. Caligula brought it to Rome, and it was moved here from Nero's circus by the order of Pope Sixtus V,' Rico told her. 'Apparently, it took four months to move it across Rome, and the men who moved it had to do it in silence, on pain of death.'

'Wow. That's a bit harsh. I assume that's another medieval thing, like the Mouth of Truth biting off the hands of liars?'

'Roman history's not *totally* gory,' Rico said, laughing.

'Gladiators, Nero, Caligula… I rest my case.' She spread her hands, laughing back.

They walked back into the city, stopping every so often to look at the gorgeous cakes in the windows of the *pasticcieri*. There were lilacs and orange trees everywhere, and Ella loved every second of it.

As they crossed the Tiber Ella asked, 'Can I take you to dinner tonight?'

She wanted to take him to dinner? That was a first. Normally, Rico did the asking. And normally, Rico did the paying. The only time someone else offered to treat him, there was usually an ulterior motive—an obvious one at that. Not being able to see a motive made him feel out of his depth, to the point where he was lost for words.

'Sorry. Of course you're probably busy. I assumed too much,' she said when he was silent.

'No, I'm not busy. And, yes, I'd like to have dinner with you.'

'And it's my bill,' Ella said firmly.

That was what he didn't get. He couldn't help asking, 'Why?'

'You cooked for me, that first night. Obviously I can't return the favour because I don't have access to a kitchen here, so the best I can offer is buying you a meal in a restaurant.' She smiled. 'I would say let's go to the swishest restaurant in Rome, but I'd guess you have to make a reservation months in advance, and anyway I don't really have anything suitable to wear.'

'Plus it would be incredibly expensive. Michelin stars and what have you don't come cheap,' he warned.

She shrugged. 'The money doesn't matter. Remember, I won all that money, and I'm under budget here anyway. I can afford it.'

Rico hid a smile. Ella might be planning a new career as a baker, but she still talked like an accountant.

'And anyway, it'd be a treat for me as well,' she added, as if trying to persuade him.

'I'll see what I can do,' he said. 'I have a few connections.'

She smiled. 'Thank you.'

'Let's have a coffee and I'll make some phone calls.'

He gulped his lukewarm espresso down, as usual, and made a few calls. Luckily Ella's Italian was nowhere near good enough to follow what he was saying. There was one particular restaurant he had in mind; the food was stunning, and there was always a huge waiting list to get a table. But it also happened to be owned by a very good friend of his, and if there was a chance he could call in a favour…

He was in luck. The *maître d'* also agreed to let him settle most of the bill beforehand and give Ella a much smaller bill at the end of the night, to Rico's relief. No way was he letting her pay for a meal *that* costly, lottery win or no lottery win. And sorting this out beforehand meant that he was still in control. No surprises.

'The good news is, I have a reservation for us at eight tonight,' he said when he'd finished the call. 'The bad news… Do you have a little black dress with you?'

She grimaced. 'No.'

'It might be an idea to buy one.' Normally, he'd just go to the Via Condotti with his current girlfriend and let her loose in the designer shops with his credit card. But he had a feeling that Ella would refuse to let him buy her a dress and shoes. And if he explained that he could afford it— and could more than afford to take her out to one of the fanciest restaurants in Rome every night of the week—he had a feeling that she'd react badly. She'd told him at the park that she didn't like lying or game-playing. Though he wasn't playing games—merely taking the chance to be seen for who he was, for once, rather than for what he stood for. And surely one little white lie wasn't that bad?

'Can you recommend any shops?' she asked.

'It depends what you want. The big designers have shops on the Via Condotti.'

She wrinkled her nose. 'Sorry, I'm not really a designer person. How about something...well, not cheap and cheerful, but not ridiculous designer prices, either?'

He loved the fact that she was so no-nonsense. And he'd just bet that she shopped efficiently, rather than dragging round every shop and then going back to the first one at the end of a long, miserable day. 'Sure. Let's go.'

Rico discovered that he'd underestimated her on the efficiency front. 'Colour me impressed,' he said. 'I've never met a woman who could choose a dress *and* shoes all within the space of twenty minutes.'

Ella frowned. 'That's incredibly sexist.'

'No. It's based on painful experience,' he said with a grimace.

'You've been dating the wrong kind of woman,' she teased.

Now he'd met Ella, he was beginning to think that himself. Which was ridiculous. He didn't want a relationship; he'd seen first-hand just how messy things could get, and he never wanted to be in that position himself. But there was something about Ella Chandler. Something he couldn't put his finger on. Something that drew him and scared him at the same time.

They bought cold drinks at a *caffè* and sat watching the world go by for a while, relaxing in the sun.

'Our table's booked for eight,' Rico said. 'So I'll have a taxi ready for us at seven-thirty and I'll pick you up at your room.'

'That'd be great. Thanks.'

He saw her back to the hotel, then sat on his terrace for a while, thinking about Ella. It would've been nice to share the fading afternoon with her here, but the explanations would be way too complicated.

He showered, shaved and changed into a suit, then went to meet Ella. When she opened the door to him, he whistled in appreciation. She'd chosen a very classic black dress and plain high-heeled court shoes: simple, but very effective. 'You look lovely.'

'Thank you.' She blushed prettily. 'You look nice, too.'

'Mille grazie.' He bowed his head in acknowledgement of the compliment. 'Shall we go?'

At the restaurant, he had a rapid conversation with the *maître d'* in Italian to make sure that what he'd arranged that afternoon still stood; and then they were shown to their table. Just what he'd asked for; it was right by the plate-glass windows with a view over the city.

Watching her pay the bill didn't sit well with him, but he could see that she wanted to do something nice for him, so he smiled. 'Thank you. That was a real treat.'

'My pleasure. I'm glad I shared it with you. And the food was fabulous.'

Rico itched to take her to his rooftop garden again and dance with her in the starlight, but he contented himself with taking a taxi back to the hotel and making love to her in the big, wide bed of the honeymoon suite until they were both satiated and drowsy.

'So tomorrow, you go home,' he said, lying with her curled in his arms.

'My flight's at four in the afternoon.'

'Which means you need to check in by two, so you need to leave here at, say, one,' he mused aloud. 'You can leave your luggage here—the staff can put it in secure storage until you're ready to collect it—and I'll drive you there myself.'

'Are you sure?'

'Very sure.' He kissed her. 'And maybe tomorrow I can show you a bit of underground Rome.'

'The catacombs, you mean?'

'They're a bit of a way out of the city. No, it's a church just round the corner from the Colosseum. There's a Roman house in the basement, and you can actually hear the river running past as you walk through the rooms.' He smiled. 'And then I guess you'd like a last look at the Colosseum before we go to the airport and grab something to eat.'

'That all sounds great.'

'And I'd better let you get some sleep. *Buona notte, bellezza.* Sleep well.'

He lay awake that night, thinking about Ella. On paper, he knew it was completely crazy; they lived in different countries and she was just about to start a business venture that would take up all her time and then some. But she'd made him feel like nobody else had made him feel, and he wanted to get to know her more. To explore where all this was coming from. To find out why she was affecting him this way.

He just had to find the right words to tell her who he really was, and that he'd been a little economical with the truth. Hopefully she'd understand that he hadn't been trying to hurt her or cheat her; he'd just wanted her to see him for himself, not as Rico the hard-headed businessman or Rico the boyfriend with deep pockets. Then maybe, just maybe, they could find the time to explore where this was taking them.

* * *

After breakfast, Ella finished packing and headed down to the hotel reception area to organise leaving her luggage in their secure storage area. Rico was already there, though he was busy talking to some of the other hotel staff. They were speaking rapid Italian, so she didn't have a clue what they were saying; but something struck her as odd. The hotel receptionist seemed very deferential when she was talking to him. Given that Rico was a tour guide, surely his status would be the same as that of the receptionist? They were colleagues, not boss and employee.

And then she heard the receptionist say, '*Sì*, Signor Rossi.'

That was definitely deferential. Why wasn't the receptionist calling him by his first name?

'May I help you, *signorina?*' the other receptionist asked.

'I—um, yes. *Grazie.* I'd like to check out.'

'Of course.' The receptionist sorted out the bill and gave Ella an extra receipt for the city tax.

'May I ask…who's that man over there?' Ella gestured over to Rico, who was still earnestly in conversation with the other receptionist.

'Signor Rossi. He's very easy on the eye, no?' The receptionist smiled.

Yes. Rico was very easy on the eye. But this was the second person to use his formal name rather than his first name. Rossi. Something rang a bell there, and she couldn't remember why. 'Who is he?' she asked.

'The CEO of Rossi Hotels. We have three sister hotels in Rome,' the receptionist explained, 'though Signor Rossi is based here.'

Rico owned the hotel.

So he wasn't a tour guide at all. He'd lied to her. Ella felt sick. How rubbish was her judgement? Even for a casual fling that wasn't supposed to matter, she'd managed to find herself someone who lied. So much for the promise she'd made her mother at her deathbed. *Promise me you won't make the same mistakes I did, Ella.* Ella had promised. And what had she done? She'd planned to marry a cheat and a liar. OK, so she'd found out the truth in time to stop her making it worse and actually marrying Michael, but here she was in Rome, making the same mistake all over again; having a fling with a handsome, charming and faithless man—someone who'd lied to her right from the start.

What an idiot she'd been. Stupid, naïve and oh, so gullible. She'd thought she'd connected with him—that she knew him. But she hadn't known him at all.

Well, she'd had more than enough lies in her life. And lying was the one thing she couldn't forgive or forget: her own, very personal, hot button. If Rico could lie over something as unimportant as his job, what else would he lie about? Had he lied about being single, too? Was that why he'd never suggested spending the night with her— because he'd gone home to his partner?

The idea made her feel sick. And she really, really wanted to go home. Right now.

'Would you be able to order me a taxi, please?' she asked the receptionist. 'To the airport?'

'Of course, *signorina*. What time would you like it?'

'Now, please.'

'*Sì*, of course. Would you like to wait in the lounge, round the corner? I'll come and find you as soon as your taxi arrives.'

'*Grazie.*' With one last look at Rico—the man who'd made her feel like a million dollars, yet had lied to her consistently—Ella went into the lounge.

Please let the taxi be quick.

* * *

It was the first time Rico had ever regretted living at the flagship hotel in the Rossi chain. Normally he didn't mind dropping everything to sort out a problem with a difficult guest. But why did it have to be now?

Stupidly, he hadn't taken a note of Ella's mobile phone number, so he couldn't call her to tell her he was going to be a little late. 'Mr Banks is waiting for me in his room, yes? I need you to stall him for three minutes, Gaby, while I make a phone call,' he said.

'Will do,' Gabriella said, looking relieved. 'Thank you, Signor Rossi.'

'Prego,' he said politely, trying not to show his irritation.

He rang Ella's room; there was no answer. So either she was still having breakfast in the hotel's restaurant or she was in the shower, he guessed.

'Gaby, can I ask you to get a message to Signora Chandler for me? She's in the honeymoon suite. Tell her I've been delayed, and I'll be with her as soon as I can. If she'd like coffee, whatever, then it's on the house, OK?'

'Of course, Signor Rossi,' the receptionist said.

Rico took a deep breath and summoned a smile. From what Gabriella had told him, Mr Banks sounded like the kind of guest who'd complain if he couldn't find something to complain about. But, all the same, he was a guest and deserved courtesy and attention. Hopefully Rico would be able to sort out all the misunderstandings—and then Ella would be waiting for him.

Ella sat in the back of the taxi, barely paying any attention to her surroundings as the driver took her through the outskirts of Rome and onto the motorway towards the airport.

Why had he lied to her? That was what she didn't understand. Why had he pretended to be somebody else? Was he so rich, spoiled and bored that he got his kicks from making a fool out of people?

What an idiot she'd been, letting herself fall for every word he'd said. Accepting everything at face value. She really ought to have known better. The man she'd spent three days with—the man she'd let into her bed and started to let into her heart—just didn't exist. Rico the tour guide was a complete fabrication. Rico the CEO was a complete stranger; she knew nothing of his true self.

As for that coin she'd thrown into the Trevi Fountain— well, she had no intention of ever coming back to Rome.

Finally, Rico left Mr Banks smiling and satisfied. The man had to be the most difficult guest he'd ever encountered— the room was too small, the towels were the wrong size and hadn't been laundered, the pillows were too flat, the bed was too hard, the air-conditioning didn't suit him, and as for the city tax that tourists had to pay on top of an already extortionate hotel bill...

Rico had listened, empathised and made suggestions. And he'd upgraded the man's room, even though he suspected that Mr Banks was the kind of customer who booked the cheapest room in every hotel he stayed at and then complained until he was upgraded to the best suite. He'd gently explained that anyone staying in Rome had to pay the city tax, and Mr Banks' travel agent should have told him when he booked that several other cities in Italy, including Venice and Florence, levied the same tax on visitors. And he'd also very politely pointed out the notice in the bathroom asking guests to help the hotel be more environment-friendly by leaving the towels that needed laundering in the bathtub and putting the ones they didn't mind re-using on the towel rack. If Mr Banks wanted all his towels laundered every day, that was fine.

He took a deep breath. At least now he could see Ella.

Except she wasn't waiting for him in the lounge next door to the hotel reception, as he'd expected. Maybe she'd missed the message and was waiting for him in her room, he thought, and rang her room. Again, there was no answer.

He frowned and went over to the reception desk. 'Gaby, did you manage to get hold of Signora Chandler?'

'Ah, Signor Rossi. I'm afraid not. She'd already checked out and left.'

What? He couldn't believe what he was hearing. Why had Ella gone without a single word to him?

'Maria booked a taxi for her.' Gabriella gestured to the other receptionist.

'A taxi?'

'To the airport.'

'Right.' He could see that Maria was busy with a guest. 'Can you ask her to come to my office for a quick word when she's free?'

'Of course, Signor Rossi.'

'Thank you,' he said, keeping a lid on the hurt and anger that threatened to bubble over, and headed for his office.

'Rico? I thought you were taking three days off?' Lina said when he walked through the door.

'I changed my mind.' Warning her silently not to ask, he closed his office door behind him.

Ten minutes later, there was a rap on the door. 'Signor Rossi? Gaby said you wanted a word.' Maria looked worried.

'Come and sit down,' he said, forcing himself to give her a reassuring smile. It wasn't her fault that Ella had left without even saying goodbye. 'I believe you booked a taxi for Signora Chandler?'

'Yes.'

'Did she leave a message for me?'

'No.' Maria frowned. 'Is something wrong?'

Yes. But how could he explain it without making himself look a fool? 'She's a friend of the family,' he fibbed. 'I was going to give her a lift to the airport this morning, but then…'

Maria rolled her eyes. 'Signor Banks.'

He should've reminded her that they should always be ultra-polite about a guest, however difficult, but he understood exactly what she meant. 'Gaby was going to give Signora Chandler the message that I'd been delayed, but she'd already left before Gaby could find her.'

'But Signora Chandler pointed you out in the lobby and asked me who you were. I told her.' Maria frowned. 'If you were giving her a lift to the airport, why didn't she know who you were?'

Oh, great. Now he was tangled in a real web of lies. His own fault, for not being honest in the first place. All he could do was bluff it out. 'Nonna knows her grandparents. We don't really know each other.' That last bit at least was true. He'd thought he knew Ella—but how wrong he'd been. 'I guess she saw I was busy and thought I might not be able to get her to the airport in time.' He smiled at Maria. 'I just wondered if she'd left me a message. But no matter. Thanks for clearing that up for me.'

'*Prego.*' Maria smiled back and left his office.

Rico leaned back in his chair. Maria had told Ella who he really was—and Ella had obviously realised that he'd lied to her. But it had been a white lie. He hadn't done it to hurt her, and she'd completely overreacted to the situation.

Perhaps it was just as well that she'd gone and they'd never have to see each other again. He could go back to his normal life. No more strange feelings that something was missing. What he'd shared with her had been good sex and nothing more. A holiday fling. He'd obviously spent too long in the sun—and that crazy idea of trying to make things work between London and Rome was just that. A crazy idea. Ella Chandler was nothing special. He didn't need her, he didn't want her, and he was perfectly happy with his life as it was.

CHAPTER FIVE

For the next three weeks, Ella was busy—more than busy. She spent her time working her way through all the local cafés and sandwich businesses to see if they wanted to stock her cupcakes, talking to managers at function rooms and taking samples of her cakes to see if they'd put her on their recommended supplier lists for celebration cake bakers, planning the launch party for Ella's Cakes, and making sure that all the invitations were sent out on time.

When she crawled into bed at night, she should've slept like the dead. Except she couldn't get Rico out of her head. Which made her even crosser with herself. Why was she thinking about a man who'd lied to her? Especially as she couldn't see a single reason for him to need to lie.

Yet still she dreamed of him. Every single night. And it was driving her crazy.

Rico couldn't get Ella out of his head. He kept telling himself that it was because she was the one who'd ended it and that usually he was the one who called it quits; it was just hurt pride making him feel that way. She wasn't anything special. He was being an idiot.

And yet he found himself brooding. He didn't even sit on his rooftop terrace any more, watching the sun go down and the lights of Rome bloom in the darkness—because all he could see was Ella and the delight on her face as she looked out over Rome.

He really needed to snap out of it. Focus. It wasn't as if he had nothing better to do. He had all the details through of The Fountain, a boutique hotel in Bloomsbury; the initial figures stacked up, so all he needed to do was go and see it for himself, see if his gut feel told him it was the right place for Rossi Hotels to expand in London.

London.

Where Ella was.

Maybe he should look her up while he was there. Then he could prove to himself once and for all that what they'd had was nothing out of the ordinary—and he could finally get her out of his head.

Julia plucked a leaflet from Ella's hand and replaced it with a glass of wine.

Ella shook her head. 'I don't need this, Ju—'

'Yes, you do. Just one sip,' Julia said. 'It'll help you relax.'

'I'm fine,' Ella protested.

'I've known you since we were ten. I know when you're panicking,' Julia said dryly. 'And you really don't need to, you know. Everyone's going to turn up and it's going to be a raging success.'

'That, or the local ducks are going to be having the biggest party in the world tomorrow morning,' Ella said gloomily.

Julia just laughed. 'The ducks don't stand a chance. Once people taste your cakes, they'll be thinking up excuses to have cakes made for them.'

Ella put the wine down untouched and hugged her friend. 'Thank you. I really appreciate your support. You know, you're the sister I never had.'

'You, too.' Julia returned the hug.

To her horror, Ella felt tears sting her eyes, and blinked hard. 'Oh, God. I've gone all wet. I'm not going to be able to do this.'

Julia patted her arm. 'Of course you are. Think about it. You've been working like crazy, totally overdoing things, so it's not surprising you're tired and feeling a bit emotional. Today's a big deal for you. Your dream's finally coming true. Take a swig of that wine and then a deep breath, and you'll be fine. And remember that you make the best cakes in the whole wide world.'

This time, Ella did as her best friend said.

'OK?' Julia asked gently.

'OK.' Ella squared her shoulders. 'Let me go through my list. Wine, soft drinks and glasses, tick. Coffee and tea, tick. Cakes, tick. Business cards on every table, tick. Display book on every table, tick. Extra supplies for filling up plates in the kitchen at the back, tick.'

'Smile, tick,' Julia added.

Ella forced herself to smile. 'Yes.'

The function room was full; people were chatting and talking and clearly having a great time. Rico noticed that there was a woman refilling the plates with beautiful cupcakes in different colours. Clearly Ella's launch party was a success and the cakes were going like—well, hot cakes.

It took him a matter of seconds to locate her. She was at the far side of the room, talking to someone and writing on a pad—or was she sketching? She looked animated, almost glowing with pleasure. A kick of desire went through him. He could remember how to make her glow even more than that…

Oh, for pity's sake. It was just sex. He hadn't slept with anyone since Ella had left Rome; he'd been too busy to date, and this was just a physical reaction to abstinence, he told himself. There was absolutely no reason why his heart should be thumping like this. And he absolutely wasn't going to give into the temptation to march over to her, sweep her off her feet and kiss her until they were both dizzy. Apart from anything else, it looked as if she was talking to a potential customer. He wasn't going to barge in and spoil the deal for her. It wouldn't be fair.

Maybe some coffee would clear his head and bring his common sense back. He went over to the tables where hot and cold drinks were being served, accepted a mug of coffee from the woman serving, and smiled appreciatively at her when she encouraged him to help himself to some cake.

He took one of the smaller cakes and the taste exploded in his mouth. Wow. He'd never eaten chocolate cake this good, before. He tried another. The ivory and deep pink two-tone icing turned out to be raspberry, the tartness of the fruit cutting through the sweetness of the icing. And the peach-coloured one was a glorious riot of passion fruit icing on a coconut base.

He was pretty sure Ella had been a very competent accountant, but she'd been totally wasted in the financial world. Being able to cook like this was a gift, and setting up this business was definitely the right thing for her to do. He ought to back off and leave her be. Except something nagged at him to stay.

Something dragged Ella's attention from her client. She glanced up briefly to see what was drawing her, and nearly choked when she saw Rico.

No, it couldn't be him. It had to be someone who looked a bit like him. He was hundreds of miles away, in Rome. And why would he come to her launch party, anyway? She hadn't invited him. And if she'd really meant anything to him—if the time they'd spent together in Rome had been more than just Rico acting a role to amuse himself—then he would've got in touch with her before now. The hotel had all her details from her booking. His silence proved what she'd learned so shockingly on that last day: that it had all been some kind of spoiled playboy's game. He wasn't interested in her. He'd made that clear. He'd lied to her when there hadn't been any need to lie.

But then he caught her eye. Raised his mug. Blew her a kiss.

And every circuit in her brain felt as if it had just fried.

This wasn't fair. Just when she really needed to concentrate, all she could think of was the way that gorgeous mouth had enjoyed every centimetre of her skin, brought her such glorious pleasure. He was breathtaking to look at, and he made her feel like no one else ever had. Which made him incredibly dangerous to her peace of mind.

She hated the fact that she couldn't tear her gaze away from him. That she still wanted him every bit as much as she'd wanted him in Rome.

She dropped her pen. Although she knew it made her look clumsy, at least it made her look away from Rico. 'I'm sorry. I'm not usually this scatty,' she said apologetically to her client. She forced herself to ignore Rico and concentrate on what she did best, planning and making cakes to delight people. Finally she had all the details of the commission, took a deposit and gave her new client a receipt. She was just putting everything in her briefcase when Rico walked over.

'Ella *bellezza,*' he said softly, his voice low and husky; in response all her hormones sat up and begged.

'What are you doing here?' she asked, trying desperately to sound cooler than she felt.

'I think we have unfinished business.'

'No, we don't.'

'You walked out on me in Rome without a word.'

Her eyes narrowed. 'You lied your face off. What did you expect, congratulations and a helium balloon?'

'I think,' he said, 'we need to talk.'

She knew what he meant by that. She'd been there before with Michael. No doubt Rico, too, thought he could exercise a bit of charm and talk her round to his point of view. Wrong. She wasn't repeating her mistakes. 'I have nothing to say to you.'

'Is everything OK?' A tall, statuesque woman appeared beside Ella and gave her a concerned look.

'It's fine,' Rico said, smiling. 'Ella's cakes are amazing. And I was about to ask her to make me a special cake.'

She was looking daggers at him, and the other woman clearly picked up the atmosphere. 'Perhaps I can help you. Ella's been on the go all day.'

'You're Ella's business partner?' he asked.

'Yes,' the woman said.

'No,' Ella said at the same time, and sighed. 'It's OK, Ju. I'll deal with this.'

'Signal me if you need me, Ella,' Julia said, and gave Rico a hard look, as if warning him to go easy on Ella or he'd have her to deal with.

'Your guard dog?' Rico asked.

'My best friend,' she corrected. 'Though, yes, she does look out for me.' She lifted her chin. 'What do you want, Rico?'

'To commission a cake.'

She narrowed her eyes at him. 'I don't have time for playing games.'

'I'm not playing games. I have a business opportunity in London. If I decide to add the hotel to my chain, then

I'll need to have some kind of opening ceremony, and that in turn means I'll need a cake for the party.'

'So that's an "if". Not a definite.' She shook her head in disgust. 'Where do you stop with the lies?'

'I haven't lied to you.'

She folded her arms. 'You told me you were a tour guide.'

'Which I was. For that day. I'm hands-on in my business. I do a stint in every job, every few months, so I can see the issues my staff face and where things can be improved for both customers and staff. The day I met you, I was a tour guide.'

'Why didn't you tell me who you really were?'

'Because.' He sighed. 'Ella, this isn't the place to discuss it.'

'You're telling me.'

'Can I take you to dinner, when you've finished here?'

'Why?'

'So you can continue with your launch party and do what you do best. And then we'll talk.'

'I...'

'We have unfinished business,' he said softly, 'and you know it, Ella *bellezza*.'

She scoffed. 'I don't think so.'

There was only one way to prove it to her. He stooped very slightly and brushed his mouth against hers in the lightest, sweetest, softest kiss. His mouth tingled where it touched hers.

She shivered, and he noticed that her pupils had dilated hugely.

'And that was barely a kiss. If I kissed you properly, Ella, neither of us would give a damn that we're surrounded by strangers. We'd both go up in flames. *That's* what I mean by unfinished.'

She swallowed hard. 'I'm working,' she whispered.

'Which is why I suggested dinner. Afterwards.'

She closed her eyes, looking defeated, and for a moment Rico really didn't like himself for the way he'd pressured her. But he hadn't done anything wrong—had he? 'Just dinner, Ella. When we've talked things through.'

She opened her eyes again. 'OK.'

'Good—and, by the way, your cakes are superb.' He couldn't resist just one taunt. 'I particularly like the passion fruit one.' He put the emphasis on *passion,* and Ella blushed to the roots of her hair.

He winked at her, and disappeared back into the crowd.

Flustered, Ella grabbed the mug of coffee she'd abandoned half an hour earlier and took a gulp of the lukewarm liquid.

'Who was that?' Julia asked, returning to her side.

'It's complicated—a long story.'

'Tell me after.'

'I'm, um, having dinner with Rico afterwards.'

'Rico. Hmm.' Julia raised an eyebrow. 'And although his English is perfect, there's a definite accent there. Would I be right in saying you met him in Rome?'

Ella felt her skin heat. 'Yes.'

'You had a fling with him?'

'Um, yes.'

Julia looked hurt. 'You never said a word to me.'

'It's complicated,' Ella said again.

'You don't have to see him if you don't want to.' Then Julia's eyes narrowed. 'Hang on. I know you've been working like crazy to get things up and running, but I remember the last time you threw yourself into work like this.'

'He didn't do a Michael on me, if that's what you're asking.'

'But he knows about your lottery win?'

Ella nodded. 'That isn't an issue.' She could guess what her best friend thought: Rico was a con-man after her money. 'Actually, the money would be small change to him. He could buy me out ten times over and still have a fortune left.'

'So if he's not after your money, what does he want?'

'Right now, I don't have a clue.' That wasn't strictly true. That kiss had told her a great deal. And it had also made her libido sit up and beg.

Why had he walked back into her life, offering her temptation? Yes, physically it was good between them. Better than it had ever been for her with anyone else. But Rico had already proved to her that she couldn't trust him. She had no idea who the real Rico was. She wasn't stupid enough to put herself back in a vulnerable position; so she'd have dinner with him—and she'd tell him to stay out of her life.

She managed to keep her focus on business for the rest of the evening, though it was a real effort; even when she couldn't see Rico, she was so aware of his presence.

Finally, the last person left the party, and she started to clear up. She could hear noises from the kitchen at the back of the function room, but Julia was in the front with her, collecting plates and mugs. So who was in the back?

She nearly dropped the crockery she was carrying when she walked into the kitchen and saw Rico with his sleeves rolled up and his hands in sudsy water. 'What are you doing?'

He rolled his eyes. 'Ask the obvious, Ella *bellezza*.'

'But...'

'The quicker you're done here, the quicker I get to spend time with you. So it makes sense for me to help you clear up.'

'I guess so.'

He frowned. 'You look exhausted.'

'She's been working crazy hours since she got back from Rome,' Julia told him.

'In that case, I won't drag you out to dinner tonight, Ella,' Rico said.

She had a reprieve?

Then he added, 'I assume you have the makings of an omelette and salad in your fridge, so I'll cook for you instead. Or order takeaway, if you'd rather.'

'I…' She was too tired to think straight. Right at that moment she didn't have a clue what to say.

He sighed. 'You really are exhausted.' He dried his hands, then took the crockery from her. 'Sit down.'

'I've still got things to clear up out there.'

'I'll do it. Don't argue.'

Before she had time to collect her thoughts, he'd made a mug of coffee for Julia and herself, finished clearing up in the function room, and was back to dealing with the huge pile of washing up.

'So how do you know each other?' Julia asked.

'We met in Rome,' Rico said.

'And you've come all this way to see Ella?' She sounded disbelieving.

'I'm in London on business,' he said. 'And I saw the details of the launch party on Ella's website. So I thought I'd drop in and say hello.'

'Hmm.'

Ella could tell her best friend was still suspicious of Rico, though the fact that he was helping to clear up without being asked had redeemed him a bit in Julia's eyes.

'Is there anything else that needs doing?' he asked when he'd finished drying the crockery and Julia had put it away.

'No.'

'Good.' He rinsed out the sink. 'Can I give you a lift home, Julia?'

'No, I'm fine—I'm only two stops away on the Tube.'

Ella blinked at him. 'You drove here?'

'No, I don't have a car in London. I called a taxi.' Rico flicked open his phone and speed-dialled a number. 'Address?' he asked.

'Here?'

'No. *Your* address.'

Of course. She was too tired to think straight. And that kiss earlier hadn't helped. She couldn't stop thinking about it, about the way he made her feel. Bad, bad idea. She mumbled her address at him.

'The taxi will be here in a quarter of an hour,' he said.

It gave them enough time to lock up.

'I think,' he said softly when they were inside her flat, 'you're too tired to talk tonight.'

'I am.'

'You look all in.' He rummaged in her fridge.

She frowned. 'What are you doing?'

'Making you something to eat.'

'I'm not hungry.'

'Tough. You need to eat to keep your strength up. Especially if you're working crazy hours.'

He made her an omelette, then sat opposite her with his arms folded until she ate it. The food was surprisingly good, but then she already knew he could cook. One thing he *hadn't* lied about.

'Aren't you having anything?' she asked.

'I'll eat later.' He flapped a dismissive hand. 'I don't usually eat until late anyway.'

He washed up her empty plate and cleared up in the kitchen. 'I'll call you tomorrow. We can do lunch, or dinner—whatever fits in your schedule.'

'What about yours?'

'I can be flexible.' He touched her cheek gently with the backs of his fingers, a sweet and cherishing gesture. 'Goodnight, Ella *bellezza*. I'll speak to you tomorrow. Sleep well.'

She was pretty sure she wouldn't. He'd just turned her upside down all over again.

And yet she was out like a light the second her head hit the pillow. The next thing she knew, her alarm was beeping crazily.

She showered and washed her hair, and was halfway through drinking a mug of coffee when the phone rang. She grabbed it without looking at the display. 'Ella Chandler.'

'*Buongiorno,* Ella *bellezza.*'

That sexy, melted-chocolate voice undid all the good that the caffeine had done in sharpening her brain again. And she hated the way her libido betrayed her like this, turning her into a puddle of hormones. A pushover. 'Good morning.'

'So, are you having lunch with me today or dinner?'

'Do we really have anything to say to each other?'

'I think we do.'

She sighed. 'Dinner, then.'

'Good. I'll pick you up at eight.'

Before she could protest, the line went dead.

She replaced the receiver. God only knew what she was getting herself into, agreeing to have dinner with him and talk. And yet there was a frisson of excitement running down her spine, and the world suddenly seemed a brighter, more vibrant place than it had since she'd come back from Rome.

'Just remember that he's a liar,' she told herself. 'OK, so he's gorgeous and I have the hots for him. But he's still a liar, first and foremost.' And she had no intention of getting hurt again. Which meant most definitely not getting involved with Rico. Not now, not ever.

CHAPTER SIX

ELLA managed to keep her mind on her work—just—but by half-past seven she was antsy. Rico hadn't given her any idea about where they were going, so she had no idea what the dress code was. She didn't possess a little black dress; the one she'd bought in Rome had gone straight to a charity shop as soon as she'd washed and ironed it.

In the end, she decided to wear one of the suits she'd worn in her office job. Formal and smart might be the way to go. A suit of armour would be better still, but a work suit would have to do.

He was as prompt as he'd been in Rome, ringing her doorbell at exactly eight o'clock. It was the first time she'd seen him wearing a suit, and he looked absolutely stunning. The dark grey material, teamed with one of his trademark crisp white shirts and a silk tie, emphasised his good looks. He was utterly breathtaking—and she *wanted*.

'You look very nice,' he said, disarming her.

'Thank you.' And why was it that, even though she knew what a liar he was, her knees still went weak when he smiled? Cross with herself for being such a pushover, she asked, 'Where are we going?'

'My hotel.'

Somewhere private. Oh, help. She remembered what happened when they were in private hotel rooms together.

'We'll talk in my room. And then we'll order dinner,' he said.

'And I get no say in this?'

He spread his hands. 'I just said we'll talk in my room.'

She narrowed her eyes at him. 'You're being bossy.'

He shrugged. 'We agreed to talk. And it makes sense for it to be the hotel; it's neutral ground, and somewhere we won't be overheard.'

She locked the door behind her and followed him out to the taxi. He didn't start a conversation, and she didn't have a clue what to say without making a fool of herself, so they remained in silence until the taxi pulled up outside a boutique hotel in Bloomsbury.

'Fountain Hotel' was etched into the glass of the doors. Definitely a link with Rome, she thought.

'Is this the hotel you're thinking of buying?' she asked as the taxi drove off.

'Maybe.'

She rolled her eyes. 'I'm hardly going to go and tell the world what your plans are and scupper your business deals, am I?'

'I guess not.'

She sighed. 'Rico, what are you doing here? I mean, with me?'

'We have unfinished business, Ella *bellezza*. And we're going to talk about it now.'

They took the tiny lift up to his room. She could still remember the last time they'd been in a hotel room together, and warmth spread down her spine at the memories. Maybe this wasn't such a good idea and she should've insisted on them talking in a public place. Then again, what they were going to discuss was definitely something best done in private. She didn't want anyone else overhearing what a fool she'd made of herself.

When Rico opened the door and ushered her in, Ella was relieved to discover that he'd booked a suite rather than a room. Without a bed in sight, she might just be able to concentrate.

He offered her a seat on one of the sofas. 'Coffee? Something cold? A glass of wine?'

'I'm fine, thanks.' She stared levelly at him as he sat down on the opposite sofa. 'So, where do we start?'

'We can start with why you walked out on me in Rome.'

'You know why. I found out you'd lied to me. I don't like liars.' She lifted her chin. 'Why did you lie to me about who you were, Rico? You let me believe you were a tour guide.'

'Which I was, for that day.'

'Why couldn't you have told me the truth later that evening, when we went out to dinner?'

A muscle twitched in his cheek. 'Because you would've changed.'

She frowned. 'How?'

'Instead of seeing me for who I am, you would've seen me as the CEO of Rossi Hotels.'

She frowned. 'And what difference does that make?'

'You befriended a tour guide, a man you thought didn't have any money. You responded to me as a man. You liked me for who I was, not for my status.'

She looked at him. 'You once told me you thought I'd been seeing the wrong sort of man. It sounds to me as if you've been seeing the wrong kind of woman.'

He rubbed a hand across his eyes. 'Maybe.'

'And, actually, I'm a bit insulted that you think I could be that shallow. I don't judge people by the balance in their bank account.'

He flushed a dull red. 'I'm sorry. I didn't mean it personally. It's just how people always reacted to me in the past.' He raked a hand through his hair. 'I'm making a mess of this. Ella, what I'm trying to say is that I liked who I was when I was with you. I liked the way you made me feel, and I wasn't ready to give that up.'

'But you thought I was shallow enough to respond differently to you once I found out who you were.' She grimaced. 'I'm not sure if that's worse than what I thought originally.'

'Which was?'

She shrugged. 'That you were a bored, spoiled rich kid, and you were slumming it with me—having a joke at my expense.'

'And now you've insulted me,' he said. 'Rich, yes; spoiled, possibly; but bored and slumming it—no way. I never laughed at you, Ella. Far from it.' He gave her a wry smile. 'The irony of it is that I was going to tell you about my real job, that last day. Neither of us wants to get involved; neither of us has time for a relationship. But we're good together. So I was going to suggest that we found a way to juggle things and carry on our fling a little longer.'

She stared at him, stunned. That was the last thing she'd expected to hear.

'OK, so I was a bit evasive about my background.'

'A *bit?*'

'But you're overreacting. It really wasn't that big a deal.'

'Lying's a big deal to me,' she said. 'If you can lie about something small, what's to stop you lying about something else? How do I even know you're single and you're not just turning on the charm? I can't trust you.'

'I'm single. I wouldn't lie about that. I don't like cheats.' He looked thoughtful. 'Who lied to you so badly, Ella? Your ex?'

'Yes. And I was too stupid to see it.'

'You're not stupid,' he said softly. 'But if he was plausible, offering you what you thought you wanted, then maybe it was easier for you not to ask questions or look for problems.'

'Gullible, then.'

'Don't be so hard on yourself.' He took her hand. 'What happened?'

'I…' Bile rose in her throat at the memory. She didn't want to drag it all up again, have the top of her scars ripped open.

As if he guessed her thoughts, he said gently, 'It's not good to bottle things up. It means you don't get the chance to heal.'

He had a point. And maybe if she explained, told him the truth, it would take some of the pain away. Rico had made her feel beautiful in Rome, wiping out the hurt Michael had left. Maybe telling him the rest would help her put it where it belonged—in the past.

'I spent three years supporting Michael while he studied for his PhD. I thought we loved each other.' How naïve and trusting she'd been. 'And I knew he was working hard, juggling his thesis with his teaching commitments, so I decided to surprise him with lunch at the university. I wanted to make him feel good, give him a break. Except he was busy having…' Her breath caught. 'Let's just say he was having a very *private* tutorial with one of his students. And I walked right into the middle of it.'

'How awful for you.' Rico looked sympathetic. 'I take it you had no idea that he was cheating on you?'

'None at all. I thought he loved me.' She swallowed hard. 'But he was just using me; I was someone to pay the rent and the bills. I don't think she was the first of his students he'd had an affair with. And he said afterwards that it was my fault. That I wasn't woman enough to satisfy him.'

'That was his biggest lie,' Rico said. 'It wasn't your

fault at all. He tried to blame his own inadequacies on you.' He pressed a kiss into her palm and folded her fingers over it, and Ella had to swallow hard to stop a sob breaking through at his gentleness. 'You're woman enough, all right. He was the one with the problem.' His eyes narrowed. 'Now I understand what you mean about grovelling letters once he found out about your lottery win. I'm glad you didn't fall for it and take him back.'

'No, because I already knew I couldn't trust him. But I'm still a gullible idiot. I fell for all the lies you told me. That flat you said you borrowed…'

'I borrowed it from myself,' he said. 'I know that's equivocating, and I apologise for that.'

'And you own that swish restaurant, too?'

'No. But I admit that I'm good friends with the owner. We went to school together. So, yes, I traded on our friendship. He found me a table that night.'

'And charged me lower prices, too?' She narrowed her eyes at him. 'I didn't really think about it at the time, but when my credit card bill came through I realised it seemed a bit low for such a posh restaurant.'

Rico sighed. 'OK. I admit I settled part of the bill in advance. I knew it would be expensive and I didn't want to take advantage of you.'

There at least he wasn't like Michael, who'd really taken advantage of her. All the same, it annoyed Ella that Rico had made a high-handed decision without even discussing it with her. 'Don't you think that's just a tiny bit patronising? I told you I could afford it.'

'I know. But it still felt like taking advantage of you.' He wrinkled his nose. 'I'm sorry. I didn't mean to be ungrateful. I guess I'm used to being the one who pays.'

'So you're a control freak?' she asked. 'Except…' She shook her head. 'No, that's not what you were like. Not that first night. When you made all that effort and cooked dinner for me yourself. And you admitted that you're rubbish at puddings so you bought them from the deli.' She narrowed her eyes at him. 'You were telling the truth then, weren't you?'

'Yes. And I really was a tour guide, that day, Ella. Another time, you might've met me as a waiter. Or the male equivalent of a chambermaid.'

She blinked. 'You really clean hotel rooms?'

'And other jobs. I've worked in the kitchen—I probably have the same kind of food hygiene qualifications you do.'

'But you're the CEO of the chain.' She didn't understand. He was the boss. Why was he taking on other roles?

'That's precisely why I do it. Working a short stint in every role is the best way of seeing what issues my staff face, and it also helps me see what would make life better for my guests and for my staff. And my staff respect me for it, because they know I'm not just issuing orders from some ivory tower—they know I've done the job myself, so I'm talking from experience rather than some half-baked theory. And they also know that because I've done it myself, I appreciate what they do.'

'That figures. And the girl who told me about you seemed to respect you.'

'Good.' He paused. 'You overreacted, Ella. I told you one little white lie.'

'It was still a lie.'

'But it wasn't meant to hurt you. Your ex really messed with your head,' he said. 'Or is there more to it than that?'

'He isn't the only one who lied to me,' she admitted. 'Lying is a definite deal-breaker where I'm concerned.'

'Supposing I promise never to tell you anything but the truth, the whole truth, and nothing but the truth, from this moment on?' he asked.

She grimaced. 'You make it sound as if I'm putting you on trial.'

'Isn't that what you're doing?'

He was the one who'd lied. How come she was the one who felt guilty? She sighed. 'Rome—you and me—that was meant to be just fun. A fling.'

'Absolutely. Three days of enjoying each other's company, and we'd never have to see each other again.'

'But now you're here in London.'

'On business.'

'So why did you look me up?'

'To prove something to myself.'

'What?'

He shrugged. 'Doesn't matter.'

He really didn't like talking about himself, did he? He sidestepped questions, or even stonewalled them. She didn't have a clue what was going on in his head. She frowned. 'Where are you going with this? Rico, I'm just starting up my business. Right now I barely have time to sleep.'

'I didn't,' he said softly, 'have sleeping in mind.'

Pictures bloomed in her head, and heat coiled deep in her belly. 'Oh.' Her voice sounded husky, and she was furious with herself for giving herself away like that. She still had the hots for him. Which was crazy, because in some ways he was more of a stranger to her now than he'd been when she'd met him.

'I don't have time for this, either,' he said. 'I have an empire to finish building.'

'That's the dream you wouldn't tell me about in Rome? To build an empire?' She paused. 'Or a dynasty?'

He scowled. 'Not a dynasty. I don't want a family.'

He sounded a little too emphatic. She remembered he'd

said he wasn't close to his family. 'What's so bad about your family?'

'Let's just leave it that they want different things from me.'

'But surely your mum and dad are proud of you? You don't look much older than I am, and you're already CEO of a chain with four hotels in Rome.'

'Sounds as if you've been doing research on me.'

'No. Your receptionist told me about the other hotels. And you're avoiding the question.'

He shrugged. 'I have no idea whether my parents are proud of me and I don't actually care. I barely speak to them, and it suits all of us that way.' He looked her straight in the eye. 'What about you? I know you lost your mum—but if she'd been here I'd bet she would've been really proud of you last night. But what about your dad, your grandparents? Were they there at the launch?'

'My mum was a single parent, and…' She grimaced. 'I don't have a family to be close to. But I have good friends. That's enough for me.'

'Me, too.' He gave her a wry smile. 'Something else we have in common.'

'We're from different worlds. You're—'

'—a bored, spoiled rich kid, slumming it?' he cut in.

She blew out a breath. 'I apologise for that. But you do come from a wealthy background. I don't. My lottery win would be small change to you, but it's absolutely life-changing for me.'

'You're the one who said money isn't important,' he reminded her.

'It isn't what you have that matters; it's the kind of person you are and how you treat others that's important.'

'That works for me,' he said. 'So. You and me.' He drew her hand up to his mouth. His lips were warm against her palm. She closed her eyes as his mouth moved to her wrist; she knew he would be able to feel just how hard and how fast her pulse was beating.

'Ella *bellezza*.' He stroked her cheek and she opened her eyes again. 'Neither of us has time for this. Neither of us is looking for this. But can you honestly tell me that you want to walk away from this?'

'Honestly?' She thought about it. 'No.' She reached up to trace his lower lip with the tip of her forefinger. He had such a beautiful mouth. A mouth that had given her so much pleasure.

He drew the tip of her finger into his mouth and sucked, hard.

Lust curled through her again. 'Rico.' The word felt as if it were poured through sand.

And then they were kissing each other, hot, hard, open-mouthed. He scooped her onto his lap and slid his hands under her jacket; she could feel the warmth of his palms against her skin through the soft cotton of her shirt. Then he tugged her shirt out of her waistband and they were skin to skin. His fingertips moved in tiny circles against her skin, arousing her further. Slowly, slowly, he moved his hands from her back to her midriff, and then upwards so he could cup her breasts. She ached for his touch.

As if he read her mind, he moved one hand so he could unbutton her shirt, then stripped her jacket and shirt off at the same time.

'Your skin's so soft.' He traced the lacy edge of her bra. 'And I need to see you.'

'Yes.' She wanted this as much as he did. Needed it. He might be a liar, a man she could never trust, but he made her body sing.

He unsnapped her bra with one hand, slid the straps down, then tossed the lacy garment away. She closed her eyes and tipped her head back as he kissed his way down her throat—hot, open-mouthed kisses, swirling his tongue against her skin. Her hands slid back into his hair, urging him on.

He opened his mouth over one nipple and sucked; a bolt of pure pleasure lanced through her. But it wasn't enough. She knew he could give her more, and she wanted everything he could offer. Every touch, every caress, every taste.

When he released her, she dipped her head and kissed him.

He was shaking when he broke the kiss. 'Ella, if we don't stop now…'

'If we do stop,' she said, 'I think I might implode.'

'Me, too.' His eyes were very dark, and his accent was more pronounced.

She slid off his lap and got to her feet, expecting him to lead her through to his bedroom. But, to her shock, when he stood up, he scooped her into his arms and carried her through to his bed.

'Caveman tendencies?'

'Absolutely. And that means I want your hair down. Spread across my pillow. While I'm buried inside you.'

Oh, God, the pictures that put in her head.

That silenced her, and he laughed. 'Careful what you wish for, Ella *bellezza*.'

His smile gave her the courage to say what she was thinking. 'Right now I wish,' she said, 'that you weren't wearing quite so much.'

He set her down on her feet. 'OK, I'm in your hands. Do what you will.'

Her hands were trembling slightly as she undid the buttons of his shirt. Then she had to deal with his tie. It had been years since she'd dated a man who wore a tie— Michael had always gone for the casual college professor look—and this one felt like silk. Designer. 'Help?' she asked.

He dealt with the tie and his top button, and shrugged his jacket off. 'Better?'

'Rico, that needs hanging up.' His jacket had felt soft and smooth, and she'd bet it cost a small fortune.

'I don't care. I just need you to take the rest of my clothes off. Preferably in the next five seconds. And you can lose your skirt, first.'

She lifted her chin. 'Bossing me about, are you?'

He spread his hands and gave her the sexiest grin she'd ever seen. 'Just making a suggestion. Which you can choose to accept…or not.'

'So this thing between us—it's equal.'

'It's equal.' He narrowed his eyes at her. 'So will you just stop talking and kiss me?'

'A request. Polite. Ish,' she said. 'There's a word missing.'

He looked pained. 'Ella. *Please.*'

'Much better.' She kissed him.

Between them, they managed to get rid of the rest of their clothes, and he took the pins out of her hair. And then he lifted her up and laid her on the huge, wide bed. The mattress was firm, but the pillows were soft and deep. She drew her hand down his side, moulding her palm to the shape of his body; in return, he traced the curve of her hip and her buttocks.

'Your move,' he said, his voice deepening.

She drew one finger down his sternum and smiled.

He copied her.

She slid her hand across his midriff. Rico did the same to her, then slid his hand up to brush the under curve of her breasts. Ella closed her eyes. 'Oh, yes. More,' she whispered.

He slid his hand between her thighs to cup her sex; she wriggled, needing him closer.

At last, he drew one fingertip along her sex, teasing her until she was near to clenching her fists with frustration; her breath escaped as he pushed one finger inside her. She tipped her head back against the pillows as his thumb found her clitoris and teased it.

'You like that?' he whispered.

'Yes.' She dragged in a breath. 'But I want more.'

'Me, too.'

Ella felt the mattress dip and realised he was no longer beside her. She opened her eyes. 'Rico?'

'Condom,' he said, rummaging for his wallet and retrieving a foil packet. He ripped the packet open and rolled the latex over his shaft; the bed dipped again as he knelt between her thighs. And then at last he gently eased into her. He held still, letting her body adjust to the feel of his, then stole a kiss. 'Perfect. Just how I wanted to see you, Ella *bellezza*,' he said huskily. 'Your hair spread over my pillow, and me inside you.'

Then he began to move; he took it slowly at first, stoking her desire to fever point. Then it was as if something snapped his control and he moved faster, harder, building the pressure until finally her climax splintered through her. As her body tightened round his she could feel him tense as he reached his own release.

Finally, he eased out of her, and kissed her tenderly. 'Don't go anywhere,' he whispered as he headed for the en suite.

Alone in his bedroom, Ella felt awkward. They were supposed to be talking, sorting things out between them, and yet they'd ended up in bed. And she felt like a tart.

'What's the matter?' he asked when he came back.

She told him.

He sighed, sat on the end of the bed and took her hand. 'First of all, you're not a tart. I didn't exactly have a lot of control, either. I was with you all the way. So don't beat yourself up about it.'

'I guess.'

He drew her hand to his mouth, pressed a kiss into her palm and curled her fingers round it. 'If anything, I'm the one at fault. I was supposed to be taking you to dinner, not carrying you to my bed.' He was still holding her hand as he asked, 'So where do we go from here?'

CHAPTER SEVEN

'WHERE do we go from here?' Ella blew out a breath. 'I have absolutely no idea.'

'Let's start with what we know. Neither of us wants a relationship. Neither of us has time for one.' He paused. 'But.'

'But?'

'It's good between us. Physically.'

She narrowed her eyes at him. 'What are you suggesting?'

'I'm going to be in London for a while. Maybe we can see something of each other while I'm here.' He paused. 'Kind of friends with benefits.'

'We're not friends. We barely know each other,' she pointed out.

'Acquaintances with benefits, then.'

'You're really compartmentalised, aren't you?'

He shrugged. 'It tends to make life easier.'

'So what you're offering me is sex. Just while you're in London.'

'That sounds tacky.'

'But that's what it boils down to.'

'I guess. We're both busy and neither of us wants to get involved.' Honesty compelled him to add, 'But there's something between us.' Ever since she'd left Rome, he'd told himself that she was nothing special. Seeing her again was supposed to prove that.

Except it hadn't.

Not that he was prepared to admit quite that much to her.

And maybe seeing more of her would make this thing burn itself out. He'd get bored, the way he always did. And it would end before it stopped being fun. Before it started being serious.

'What do you want, Rico?' she asked.

He wasn't sure he could answer that. He knew what he'd always thought he wanted—to be in sole charge of the business. Which he was. And the fact that it wasn't enough for him any more, that expanding into London excited him less than the thought of seeing her, made him antsy. He threw the question back at her. 'What do *you* want?'

'You're not supposed to answer a question with a question.'

'What do you want?' he repeated.

She sighed. 'I don't know. I thought I'd got you out of my system. Tonight was supposed to be closure. And look what happened. I'm naked and in your bed.'

He already knew she felt bad about that. Which made it easier for him to admit, 'It was completely mutual.'

'So do we walk away from each other now?'

His head was telling him to run like hell. His heart was telling him to stick around. 'Do you want to walk away?'

'It would be the sensible thing to do.'

The 'but' was loud and clear. She felt the same way he did. Mixed up and torn between the options. Safe and not safe.

'I'm sorry I wasn't honest with you right from the start,' he said.

'I guess you had your reasons for what you did. I think

they're ridiculous reasons, but I suppose you weren't doing it out of a sense of meanness.'

'No, I wasn't. It's the way people are with me—they see me in terms of what I can do for them. With you, it felt different. I didn't want that to change.' She looked so cute, and he was so, so tempted just to lean forward and steal a kiss. But he held himself back. Just. 'I really ought to go and find your clothes, let you get dressed, and take you down to dinner. But I have a feeling that they're going to be pretty crumpled—just as mine are.'

'I didn't think of that.' She bit her lip. 'Everyone's going to look at us in the restaurant when we walk in and jump to conclusions. Worst of all, they're going to be right.'

'Let's order room service. We can eat in the other room. And it means we can try talking again, without an audience.'

'OK. That sounds good.'

He handed her the menu. 'Have a look through and choose what you want.'

He disappeared into the living room, then came back a few moments later with her clothes neatly stacked in a pile, which he placed on the chair. Shortly afterwards, she heard the shower running. He emerged from the bathroom wearing only a towel wrapped round his hips; she wasn't sure whether it was his near-naked body or his smile that made her heart skip a beat.

'Help yourself to whatever you need in the bathroom,' he said. 'By the way, I had a word with Reception. The hotel laundry service can press your stuff for you while we're having dinner.'

Ella felt the colour bloom in her face. 'Oh, God. So they know what we've—'

'It doesn't matter,' he cut in softly. 'We're not the first people who've got a bit carried away and we won't be the last. Anyway, for all they know, you spilled something over your jacket and skirt and had to sponge your suit down.'

She knew he was trying to make her feel better. But it didn't quite work. 'Mmm,' she said.

'Look, there's a robe behind the bathroom door. You're very welcome to use that until your suit's ready. Have you decided what you'd like from the menu?'

'The salmon, please. And can I be greedy and have the chocolate-dipped strawberries for pudding?'

'Great idea.' Though the suddenly heated expression in his eyes told her that he had ideas about the strawberries. Ideas that involved her.

Ella almost, almost climbed out of bed, removed his towel and dragged him into the shower with her. But sense prevailed—just—and she waited until he'd left the bedroom before heading for the bathroom.

The hotel toiletries were gorgeous, citrus-scented, and the towels were large and super-soft. When she came out of the shower, she noticed that her suit and shirt had gone. So he'd kept his word about the laundry service, then.

Dressed in the soft, fluffy bathrobe, she padded barefoot back out to the living room where Rico was waiting for her.

'Thank you for sorting out the laundry.'

'*Prego,*' he said, giving her a tiny bow.

He was fully dressed in a clean white shirt and chinos.

'You're pretty high maintenance, aren't you?' she asked.

'How do you mean?'

'You always wear a white shirt and it's always pristine. I hate to think what your laundry bill's like.'

'Don't you think I do them myself?'

'No. Because I think you've costed out how much that time's worth to you and you'd rather use that time in a more productive way,' she said.

He raised an eyebrow. 'Is that you talking as an accountant, or are you giving me the reason why you use a laundry service?'

'I do my own laundry, actually. Ironing time is good thinking time. And I'm an ex-accountant for the time being.'

'I'll try to remember that,' he said dryly.

'So you're thinking of buying this hotel?'

'It's a possibility, yes.'

'Why London?'

'Because we already have four hotels in Rome, and to have any more would mean we'd be competing against ourselves.'

'Expanding your empire into another country. *Veni, vidi, vici.* Maybe I should start calling you Julius,' she teased.

He laughed. 'London, Paris, then maybe Vienna or Barcelona. I have plans.'

'So that's your dream. To be a hotel tycoon.'

'Maybe,' he said. 'Actually, I like this hotel. There are a few tweaks I'd want to make, but I can see it fitting in with the rest of the Rossi chain. It's big enough to have every comfort, but it's not so big that it's impersonal. The staff care about the guests, and the facilities are good. And the figures stack up. It doesn't need much work to bring it in line with the rest of my hotels.'

'What if the figures didn't stack up?'

'Then I would've looked at other hotels.' He smiled. 'Like you, I have back-up plans. And, talking of your business, I meant to ask—how was your first day, post-launch?'

'Busy,' she said. 'I have a few orders for celebration cakes to take me into the next six weeks, and some regular cupcake orders from a couple of local cafés that will keep me ticking over in between.'

'If you're experimenting with different frostings, I'd be happy to lend my services as a taste-tester. You make the best chocolate cake I've ever eaten.'

'Thank you for the compliment.' She smiled. 'And I might take you up on that taste-testing thing. Provided you're totally honest with me.'

'I'm not going to lie to you again, Ella.'

'I don't mean that—I mean, being polite. Fudging the issue so you don't hurt my feelings. I need to know if something works or not. If it doesn't, then I can tweak the recipe until it does work.'

'Honest feedback's important. It's what I want from my guests, too,' he said. 'OK. It's a deal.'

Room service arrived, and the waiter served their meal at the table that Ella guessed Rico used as a desk during the day. The food was excellent, and by the end of the meal she'd lost her residual shyness and was totally relaxed in Rico's company. It really didn't matter any more that he was properly dressed and she was only wearing a bathrobe.

All the same, she was glad when her suit and shirt arrived, neatly pressed, along with their coffee.

'Don't change back into your clothes just yet. Come and sit with me,' Rico said, shepherding her over to the sofa.

She curled up next to him, resting her head on his shoulder and enjoying the warmth of his body against hers.

'Tell me about Julia,' he said.

'She's my best friend. I've known her since we were ten.'

'And she's an English teacher and film buff.'

'Yes.' Ella was surprised he'd remembered that; then again, to do what he did, Rico needed a keen eye for detail.

'You seemed very close.'

Mmm, and he'd called Julia her guard dog. 'Ju's like the sister I never had.'

'You don't have a brother, either? Your mum didn't re-marry?'

'I'm an only child. And Mum didn't marry my father in the first place.' Ella pulled away from him. Well, he might as well know what he was getting into if he planned to start seeing more of her. Even if it was supposed to be acquaintances with benefits and no emotional entanglement. 'He was already married to someone else. Mum didn't have a clue that he wasn't single until she fell pregnant with me. Then, when she told him she was expecting me, he told her that she'd have to deal with it.' She lifted her chin. 'In other words, get rid of me. Which she refused to do. So he dumped her.'

'That's appalling.' Rico winced. 'I'm beginning to see why you have a thing about lies.'

'It wasn't just Mum he lied to. It was his wife, too. And I'd bet Mum wasn't the first to fall for him—or the last.' She sighed. 'My grandparents didn't react very well to the news that she was expecting me and the baby's father didn't want to know. She was an only child—a very late baby—and they were more like her grandparents than her parents, with an older generation's views on morality.'

Rico sucked in a breath. 'Please tell me they got over it and supported her.'

'Far from it. They said they were ashamed of her. They, too, wanted her to get rid of me. When she refused, they threw her out,' Ella said grimly. 'But Mum managed to find a flat, and when I was growing up she worked three jobs to make sure she could put food on the table for both of us.'

'Which is why you wanted a safe job when you grew up.'

'Financial security.' She nodded. 'And it was fine. I could do my cakes in my spare time. I've just been incredibly lucky and now I have a chance to do what I really love and make a living from it.' She blinked away the threatening tears. 'I just wish I'd won that money when Mum was still here, so I could've treated her and made some of her dreams come true, too. And I would've bought her a flat, given her the security she always wanted and never really had.'

He frowned. 'Didn't your father have to pay her maintenance?'

'Mum wouldn't have taken it, even if he'd offered. It wasn't about the money, for her. And I'm pretty sure he didn't offer in any case. What I found when I was going through her things last year, after she died...' She grimaced. 'When I was a kid, I used to feel it that I didn't have a dad—I really envied my friends who had two parents to go home to, and who talked about their dads teaching them to swim or ride a bike. I didn't even have an uncle. But now I'm glad he's never been part of my life. I don't think he's the kind of man I'd want to know.'

'What did you find?' Rico asked softly.

'Thirty-six envelopes. Each one contained a photograph of me on my birthday or at Christmas, for every single year since I was born. And every one was marked "return to sender".' Ella tried not to grind her teeth. 'Her letters never asked him for a thing. She was only writing to let him know how I was getting on. She told him about me, and she really tried to build some kind of connection between us—but he threw it back in her face every single time. She even sent the letters to his office rather than to his home, so it wouldn't be like rubbing his wife's face in it. But he just didn't want to know.'

'Thirty-six envelopes. And you're twenty-eight?'

'Yes.'

'So he must've kept some?'

Ella shook her head. 'Mum gave up sending them when

I turned eighteen. So now you know why I don't have a family. I probably have half-siblings somewhere out there—who knows how many other women fell for the same lies that my mum did?—but they've never tried to find me, and I don't need them. I have good friends, and that makes me luckier than a lot of people.'

'Did your grandparents soften once they met you?'

'No. Mum tried to stay in touch with them, but they refused to see us. And it's too late for any reconciliation now—they both passed away, some years back.'

'It was their loss, not yours.' Rico pulled her onto his lap and held her close.

For a moment Ella thought that she saw something in his expression—something that told her he understood how she felt because he'd been badly let down himself—but he masked it so quickly that she couldn't be sure.

Sitting so close with him like this made her feel so warm, so secure. And the question slipped out before she realised what she was going to say. 'So do I get to see you tomorrow?'

'Maybe. What time do you finish?'

'I'm not sure. Late afternoon, I guess.' She thought about it. 'I have two celebration cakes to make and flat-ice, and then I need to do some of the sugar work for them, as well as make the cupcakes for the two local cafés who've agreed to stock my cakes. And there's the business admin stuff. If I keep on top of it, then it won't take long. If I leave it to pile up, it'll be a chore.'

'So the cupcakes have to be ready before the cafés open. Does this mean a really early start?'

She smiled. 'That rather depends on whether you call six a.m. early.'

'I'd better get you home, then. It's not fair to make you

burn the candle at both ends. If you want to get dressed in my bedroom, I'll call a taxi.'

'Thank you.'

The phone rang as she walked back into the living room. Rico answered it. 'That's great. Thank you very much.' He turned to Ella. 'That was Reception. They're very efficient—the taxi's here already.'

'Thank you. I guess I'll see you tomorrow, then.'

'I'll see you home. I would've driven you myself, but I haven't sorted out a car yet.'

Outside her flat, he kissed her lingeringly in her doorway.

'What time do you finish tomorrow?' she asked.

'That depends on how my meetings go.' He wrinkled his nose. 'Plus I have a pile of paperwork to get through and a few phone calls to make to Rome.'

'Call me when you're free,' she said.

'I'll do that.' He kissed her again. 'Goodnight, Ella *bellezza*. Sweet dreams.'

CHAPTER EIGHT

WHEN Ella's alarm clock went off at five-thirty the next morning, she woke with a smile on her face. This was everything she'd wanted: being her own boss, organising her own work and being responsible for everything. And she didn't mind the early starts, because she loved what she was doing.

And she loved the way her schedule was coming together. The way she was able to work at a pace to suit her, to music she enjoyed listening to, and she didn't have to change things to suit other people. Perfect.

She baked the cupcake orders for the two local cafés; while the cakes were cooling, she made the fruit cakes and put them in the oven. Once she'd iced the cupcakes, she dropped off the boxes to her clients, then came back to check on the fruit cakes and start making the sugar roses. The Madeira cake was next; finally, when all the large cakes had cooled, she flat-iced them, ready for decorating.

She'd just washed up and put the icing bowls away when her mobile phone rang.

'Hi. You asked me to call you when I was done,' Rico said.

And how crazy it was that hearing his voice made her heart beat faster. This wasn't good. 'Uh-huh.' If she had any sense left, she'd tell him she was too busy to see him. But her mouth had other ideas. 'Are you coming over now?'

'It's a good time?'

Tell him no, her common sense urged.

'It's fine. See you when you get here.'

'I'm on my way. *Ciao, bellezza.*'

Ella had just about finished tidying her kitchen when he arrived.

'Wow, you made these?' he said, looking at the sugar roses. 'They're incredibly delicate. And very realistic.'

'They're for a wedding cake—though it's one that was booked in weeks ago. Normally people book cakes like this at least six weeks in advance.'

'How fast can you do a celebration cake?'

'If it's just a normal-sized cake and I don't have to do carving or armature or lots of intricate sugar-paste work, I can do one in a day—baking it, flat-icing it and basic decoration.'

'Carving and armature?' Rico asked, looking puzzled.

'Shaped cakes. Some of them need support so they don't collapse—that's the armature bit.' She took her display book from the shelf and flicked through it until she found the page she wanted. 'Like my dinosaur.'

'This is a million miles away from what I do in my job,' Rico said. 'I wouldn't even know where to start, making something like that. And how do you get the colours on the icing?'

'I hand-paint it. It's pretty labour-intensive, but I love doing it. Creating someone's dream out of sugar, butter, eggs and flour.' She smiled at him, 'So what do you want to do this evening?'

'Are we talking acquaintances or benefits?'

To her annoyance, she actually blushed. 'Acquaintances. Rico, I hope you realise I don't sleep around.'

'Neither do I. Don't believe everything you read in the press.'

She stared at him, shocked. 'The press follow you about?'

'In Italy, sometimes. It depends who I'm seeing.'

'I'm a nobody, so you should be safe,' she said dryly.

'That wasn't what I meant. But the press blow things up out of proportion and twist a story to suit themselves. If everything they said about me was true, there'd be so many notches I wouldn't actually have a bedpost left. Dating someone doesn't necessarily mean sleeping with them.' He leaned forward and stole a kiss. 'Let's start again. What do you want to do this evening?'

Her mouth was tingling—and that kiss had been the lightest and sweetest of touches. He tempted her so badly that she could barely resist him. 'Do you want to come upstairs for a mug of coffee while we think about it?'

'Sure.' He followed her up to her flat. 'What sort of thing do you normally do in the evenings?'

'It depends what kind of day I've had.' She switched on the kettle and shook grounds into a cafetière. 'I might go to the cinema or out for a drink with friends; I might just go for a walk by the river; or I might collapse on the sofa in front of the telly.' She gave him a wary look. 'I should perhaps warn you I'm really not into clubbing.'

'Good. Me, neither.' He looked at the photographs pinned with magnets to her fridge. 'That must be your mum.'

'Yes.' She had to swallow hard. Even now, a year later, she still missed her mother badly. Missed her smile, her gentle calmness, her common sense.

'She's very like you,' he commented.

'I hope so.' She definitely hoped she hadn't inherited any of her father's genes. Pushing the thought away, she suggested, 'Maybe we can go for a walk by the river? It's really pretty here in Greenwich.'

'I'd like that. And I'd like to see more of London while I'm here. What's the epitome of London?'

She thought about it. 'I guess it'd be something like the Changing of the Guard outside Buckingham Palace. Mind you, you need to be there early to get a decent spot to see it, so it'll have to be a weekend.'

'We'll leave that for Saturday, then.'

She gave him a regretful smile. 'Sorry, I can't make it. I'm working.'

'You're working six days a week?' Rico looked concerned. 'You're risking burnout if you keep up that kind of pace.'

'Unless I have a really big celebration cake to sort out, it's only half a morning on Saturdays, enough to keep the cafés stocked with cupcakes. They're closed on Sundays, so I can take Sundays off,' she explained.

'Let's do the Changing of the Guard on Sunday, then.'

He hadn't given her any idea about his schedule; she didn't have a clue when he was going back to Rome. 'Are you in London for very long?'

'Possibly.'

Which served her right for asking a closed question. Then again, she had the feeling that Rico could turn the most open question into a closed one.

'We should make a list of places we're going to see.'

She rolled her eyes. 'You're such a control freak, Rico.'

'You work with lists,' he pointed out, gesturing to the lists held to her fridge door by magnets.

'I like being organised.'

'Now who's the control freak?' he teased, and kissed her.

If he kept this up, she'd forget all about making acquaintances and go straight for benefits. 'Busted,' she said, and moved away from him to make the coffee—while she still could. 'With you coming from Rome, I guess we should do a tour of Roman London. We can start with the Roman Wall; plus there's a Roman bath near the Strand, and an amphitheatre under the Guildhall. And guide books are bound to list other stuff I don't know about.'

'So you're going to be my personal tour guide of London?'

'Ironic, considering how I met you.' She coughed. 'Except *I'm* not pretending to be a guide.'

'I wasn't pretending. I was doing the job—and I didn't hear any complaints from you,' he reminded her.

'No. You really made the Colosseum come alive for me. You know a lot about your home city.'

'Because I love Rome,' he said simply. 'It's the only place I ever want to live.'

So this thing between them, she thought, had definite limits. She had no intention of moving to Rome, and he had no intention of moving here. Not permanently. So she'd take the warning as read. This was a fling, until his interest waned. She'd enjoy it while it lasted, but she wouldn't expect anything more from him.

He took a mouthful of the coffee she gave him. 'This is good. Thanks.'

'My pleasure.'

'Let's make that list. Do you have a laptop?'

She fetched it and placed it on the kitchen table between them. He scooped her onto his lap and wrapped his arms round her waist. 'Now we can both see the screen,' he said.

'We could both see it perfectly well from where we were sitting,' she pointed out.

'Yes, but this way is more comfortable.' He kissed the curve of her neck.

He was right; it felt good to be held close to him like this. Not that she was going to tell him. She didn't want him thinking that all he had to do was whistle and she'd sit up and beg.

Between them, and with the help of a few websites, they came up with a mixture of the famous sights and some quirky, out-of-the-way places to visit.

'Enough for now. It's a nice evening. Let's go for that walk by the river,' he said.

The sky was streaked with pink feathery clouds as they wandered hand in hand along the path by the Thames.

'Since I'm being your personal tour guide, I should tell you that that's the Royal Naval College,' she said, pointing out the complex of beautiful white buildings and the twin grey domes with their gold clocks and weather vanes. 'It was designed by Christopher Wren.'

'Like St Paul's. Which we need to add to our list,' he said. 'It's gorgeous.'

They carried on down the Thames Path until they reached a waterfront pub. 'I sometimes stop here for a drink with Ju,' Ella said. 'Apparently Dickens used to drink here. And the food's OK, too, if you fancy something to eat?'

'Sure.' They had a drink on one of the wrought-iron balconies, then headed back inside when their food was ready; the waiter had found them a table overlooking the Thames.

When they came back out, the sky was midnight blue, fading almost to white and then deep orange at the horizon, and the buildings of London were all lit up. 'That's the Millennium Dome over there,' she said, pointing out the white dome with its yellow, blue and red spikes. 'It always reminds me of a birthday cake with candles on it.'

'London's beautiful by night,' Rico said. He leaned down to kiss her. 'And so are you.'

'Thank you.' It wasn't just the words that touched Ella. Rico made her feel beautiful in the way he touched her, the way he listened to her. And he really had seemed interested in her job, not just as if he were being polite.

They walked hand in hand back to her flat.

'Do you want to come in for coffee?' she asked, unlocking the door.

'Not coffee,' he said, and dipped his head to kiss her.

By the time he broke the kiss, Ella was shaking with need. She made no protest when Rico scooped her up, pulled the door closed behind him, and carried her up the stairs to her bed. She wanted this every bit as much as he did, matching him touch for touch and kiss for kiss. And it shocked her how quickly he could make her climax. She'd never, ever experienced that kind of intensity before.

When he came back from the bathroom fully dressed, she blinked in surprise. Wasn't he going to stay?

'Not a good idea,' he said softly, as if her thoughts had been written all over her face.

'Will I see you tomorrow?' she asked, hating herself for sounding needy but wanting to know the answer.

'No. I'm up to my eyes. But I'll call you. And I'll see you on Saturday.'

'Sure.' Acquaintances with benefits. That was what they'd agreed. And she'd be a fool to want more. 'I'll see you later.'

Although Ella was busy on Friday, she was surprised to discover that she missed not seeing Rico, and the highlight of her day was when he called her.

Which was utterly ridiculous. She didn't need a man to make her life complete. Especially one who clearly wasn't going to give anything of himself.

On Saturday, Rico arrived at Ella's kitchen at half-past

eight, just when she was putting cupcakes in a box. 'What's that?' he asked, going over to the plate where a single cupcake sat. Then he laughed, seeing his name piped on top of the icing. 'Now that's cute.'

She rolled her eyes. 'You were supposed to ask if any of those cakes were going begging. And then I was going to tell you that, actually, one of them had your name on it, and present you with that one.'

He wrapped his arms round her waist and kissed her. 'I like your sense of humour, *bellezza*. Are you done, or is there anything I can do to help?'

'I'm just dropping these off at the cafés. You can be my delivery boy and carry the boxes, if you like.'

'Delivery boy, hmm? I assume the payment is in cake. But I should ask before accepting the job what the benefits package is.'

Oh, the ideas that put in her head. 'Cake,' she said firmly. She wrapped catering film over his cupcake and put it in the fridge.

He laughed and stole a kiss. 'OK. Today's "acquaintances", too. I get it. Give me the boxes, *bellezza*.'

Once they'd dropped off the cakes, they caught the Tube to Trafalgar Square. 'I used to come here with my mum to feed the pigeons when I was a little girl,' she said, 'but people are banned from feeding them now.'

'I can see why. Their droppings do a lot of damage to stonework, and they're a health hazard. I don't encourage them at any of my hotels, either,' Rico said. He gazed round the square. 'So this is the famous fountain—the one everyone jumps into on New Year's Eve?'

'Well, not everyone. And I imagine this probably feels a bit plain and small to you, after all the gorgeous ones in Rome, but it's had a makeover recently, so it's lit up by coloured lights at night. And the water goes higher now than I ever remember it being when I was a child,' she said.

'No, it's charming,' he said.

They wandered along to see the bronze Landseer lions guarding Nelson's Column. 'I like these, too. Very stately,' he said with a smile.

'We could go to the National, as we're here,' she said. 'Or, as it's a nice day, maybe we can walk by the river. There are usually street performers on the South Bank at weekends.'

'It's too nice to go indoors,' he agreed.

Over on the South Bank, there were indeed the street performers she'd promised: living statues, jugglers, a contortionist, a man making balloon animals for children, and a string quartet in full evening dress playing Mozart.

There were also a crowd of artists, sketching caricatures and portraits of willing punters. He smiled. 'They're like the ones at the top of the Spanish Steps. Rome isn't so very different from London.' He gazed up at the London Eye. 'That's on our list, yes?'

'Yes. I'm not sure whether to take you there by day or by night.'

'We'll do both.' He gave her a wicked grin. 'Seeing as I'm such a spoiled rich kid.'

She sighed. 'I did apologise for that.'

'I know. I'm angling for a kiss better.'

'Oh, you fraud.'

'Please?' He batted his eyelashes at her. 'Pretty please with sugar on it?'

How could she resist? This was a different side of Rico. A playboy, but not a selfish one. And she really, really liked this side of him. Though at the same time it made her nervous. Was this the real Rico? She couldn't tell; and it worried her how easy it would be to let herself fall for him. How could she fall for him when she wasn't sure she could trust him?

When he saw the children playing in the fountain installation, jumping the boundaries between each 'room' made from the fountain jets when they died down, he tugged at her hand. 'Come on. That looks like fun.'

'I'm not sure if there's a set rotation of the walls or if it's random,' she said.

He watched the walls of water for a while. 'Random. Which is more fun. Your choice which way we jump—now!'

She picked the wrong one, and they both got soaked as the water rose up between the grids. Rico simply laughed and kissed her.

'Typical Roman boy—can't resist the fountains,' she teased.

They lay on the grass in Jubilee Gardens to dry out, enjoying the early summer sunshine. 'Do you like Chinese food?' she asked.

'Yes.'

'Good—we'll eat in Chinatown tonight.'

He smiled. 'I love it when you go all bossy on me.'

She coughed. 'Isn't that a bit pots and kettles?'

'A bit what?'

'Pots and kettles.' She flapped an apologetic hand at him. 'Sorry, your English is so good that I forget you might not know all the idioms. It's a saying, "the pot calling the kettle black"—because they were both covered in soot. Or were, in the days when people cooked over an open fire,' she explained.

'Hypocritical, you mean. As in me calling you bossy when I'm just as bad.'

'Yes.'

He leaned over and kissed her until she was dizzy.

'If we weren't in a public place, I'd show you just how bossy I can be,' he whispered.

He'd actually made her forget where they were. And that people were all round them—people who could see him kissing her so passionately, and the way she responded to him. Colour rushed into her face, and he laughed. 'I love the way you blush. You're so cute, Ella *bellezza*. And you're like nobody else I've ever met.'

'I hope that's meant in a nice way.'

'Yes.' And Rico was surprised by how much he was enjoying Ella's company. He could relax with her, be himself, act on crazy impulses and play in a fountain with her—and she didn't complain that her hair was ruined or sulk about getting splashed. He was enjoying himself more than he had in years.

Yet, at the same time, it made him panic. It would be, oh, so easy to fall for Ella Chandler. To be hers for the taking.

But what if, once he let her that close, he wasn't enough for her? Just as he hadn't been enough for his parents. Just as he wasn't enough for his grandparents.

He'd never really loved anyone. And maybe he never would be able to love someone the way that Ella would want to be loved. Maybe it just wasn't in him.

'Come on, *bellezza*. You're supposed to be showing me round London.' And he needed serious distraction from his thoughts. The best way to distract himself would be to carry Ella to his bed—sex always worked—but he'd promised not to rush her. And he had a nasty feeling that sex was different with Ella because she was something special.

Exactly the opposite of what he'd been trying to prove to himself.

* * *

They continued their tour of London; in the evening, she took him to a restaurant in Chinatown. The incredibly abrupt waiter waved them downstairs, where another waiter sat them on a large table with several complete strangers, then banged down a pot of jasmine tea and two handle-less cups in front of them.

'The service here won't have the finesse you're used to,' she said, 'but I promise the food makes up for it. They do the best crispy duck in London.'

'It's an experience, I'll give you that,' Rico said with a grin.

'And we're going halves on the bill. Equals, remember.'

'*Sì, signorina.*' He dipped his head and gave her a deferential look. She rolled her eyes and punched his arm, and he just laughed.

After their meal, they wandered back through Leicester Square.

'I don't know if I dare suggest stopping here for an ice cream. Not when Italian ice cream is the best in the world,' Ella said, looking longingly in the window of one of the ice-cream shops.

'If you want an ice cream, *bellezza,* that's fine. Though I'll pass, because I happen to know there's a cupcake with my name on it in your fridge and I want to make sure I can do it justice.'

They caught the DLR back to Greenwich, and she produced the cupcake from the fridge. 'Enjoy.'

He savoured every mouthful. 'I'm seriously thinking about kidnapping you and making you my personal pastry chef.'

'So I'd cook at your whim?'

'No. You can cook whatever and whenever you like. Your pleasure will be mine.'

It was suddenly hard to breathe, because she knew he

wasn't just talking about food. And he had a point. She got a real kick out of pleasing him; and it was entirely mutual.

As if he guessed at her thoughts, he drew her towards him. He kissed her until she forgot what day it was, then brought her to an incredibly intense climax before taking it much more slowly and doing it all over again.

Curled up in bed beside him, her head resting on his shoulder, she asked softly, 'So are you staying tonight?'

Stay.

Rico was shocked by how much he wanted to take her up on that offer.

But this really wasn't a good idea. Sex was one thing, but intimacy was quite another. Dangerous. He still didn't want his heart involved. And she was vulnerable; he was pretty sure that most of her assertions were utter bravado and what she really wanted was a family. Something he'd never be able to give her.

Gently, he disengaged himself from her. 'Sorry. I've skived off all day, so I'll have a pile of emails waiting for me when I get back to the hotel,' he said. He knew he was using his business as an excuse, but he didn't want to hurt her. 'But I'll see you tomorrow.' He smiled to soften his words. 'My personal tour guide promised me the Changing of the Guard.'

'Buckingham Palace is nearer you than me, so I'll meet you at The Fountain,' she said.

'Fine. What time?'

'Is nine o'clock too early?'

'Nine o'clock is fine. I'll see you then.'

Ella hid her disappointment that Rico didn't stay. This was a fling and nothing more. So why did she feel so empty as soon as he was gone…?

* * *

On Sunday, Rico was waiting in the reception area of The Fountain when Ella walked in. '*Buongiorno*, Ella *bellezza*,' he said.

'Good morning. Are you ready to play tourist?'

'Absolutely.' He gave her a wide smile.

They were near enough to walk to the palace from his hotel, and eventually joined the queue of people waiting outside Buckingham Palace. At last, the soldiers in their red tunics and tall bearskin hats marched onto the forecourt outside the palace, and he enjoyed watching the spectacle. Though he had a nasty feeling that, more than that, what he was really enjoying was being with her.

She smiled at him when it was over. 'So there you have it. One very British tradition.'

'Nothing like you'd see in Rome. You might get the odd Roman legion and a bunch of senators in the Circus Maximus on a weekend—usually re-enactment groups—but I've not seen anything like this before.'

'I'm glad I've shown you something new.' She laced her fingers through his as the old guard marched away. 'You showed me the grisly bits of Rome. It's time I returned the favour—we'll go and see the Tower of London.'

'So is this the oldest building in London?' he asked as they walked inside the complex.

'Just about,' she said. 'Though your Colosseum's a thousand years older. William the Conqueror started it with the White Tower, and various kings extended the buildings over the years. I remember my mum taking me here when I was small; I was fascinated by the Beefeaters and their hats. And the ravens.'

'Let's go and see the ravens,' he said.

The ravens stalked across a patch of ground by the Wakefield Tower. 'According to legend, the kingdom and the tower will fall if the ravens fly away, so their wings are clipped to make sure they don't,' Ella told him.

'Poor things. They're trapped.' Which was how he'd felt at university. He'd been groomed to take over Rossi Hotels, so he knew that choosing any other career would mean letting his family down; his father was totally useless, and Rico was the only grandchild. The only one who could continue the business. Without him, hundreds of jobs would be at risk, and that wasn't fair on the staff who'd worked for Rossi Hotels for years.

Yet it wasn't fair on him, either, to have all his choices taken away. Frustration at being hemmed in had nearly sent him off the rails; and then his best friend had pointed out that, actually, the world was at his feet because he could take the business in any direction he liked and he didn't have to follow his grandfather's lead.

Which was precisely why his next hotel was going to be in London rather than in Italy. He was in charge, and he was putting his stamp on the firm. And this deal was going to be a lot bigger than the last one he'd made. He was branching out, in more ways than one—and he already knew his grandfather had reservations about it. Well, tough. Rico didn't have reservations. He was going to make this work. And then maybe his grandfather would be forced to admit that Rico was doing just fine.

'The ravens' wings are almost the same colour as your hair,' she said, ruffling it.

He caught her round the waist, spun her round and kissed her; she was pink and laughing by the time he'd finished.

'Now, now. You're not supposed to distract the tour guide,' she scolded, but she was laughing as she spoke.

'How long is it since you've been here?' he asked.

'I'm not sure. Years. But I loved it as a child. The crown jewels, Henry VIII's armour…'

'What's the significance of the polar bear?' Rico asked, gesturing to the sculpture.

'There used to be a menagerie here. Actually, there's sort of a Roman connection, because the Holy Roman Emperor Frederick II sent Henry III three leopards when Henry married Frederick's sister Eleanor. It really snowballed from there; the King of Norway sent Henry a polar bear.' She smiled. 'My mum told me how the bear was kept on a long leash so he could swim in the Thames and catch fish. And then the King of France sent Henry an elephant. Apparently it came up the Thames by boat. Mum and I made up a song together about elephants in the tower, but I can't remember how it goes now.'

How different from his own childhood. He could barely remember either of his parents taking him out; they certainly hadn't told him endless stories or made up songs with him or spent time with him, the way Ella's mother had with her. Materially, Ella's childhood had been poor, but she'd had more than enough love to make up for it. Given the choice between being spoiled and being loved, that was what he would've wanted too; but he didn't think either of his parents had known how to love anyone except themselves. Definitely not each other; and definitely not him.

And why the hell was it bothering him again now? He was grown up and over it. Plenty of people had had it far worse than he had. And he had a great life. He wanted for nothing. Don't be so pathetic, he told himself.

'Rico? Is something wrong?'

He forced himself to smile. 'Nothing, *bellezza*. So what happened to the menagerie?'

'It became London Zoo, just before Victoria became queen.'

'Is London Zoo on our list?'

'It can be.' She smiled at him. 'Anything you like.'

Her sweet, open smile made him feel as if something were cracking inside him. Like the sun shining to melt away the loneliness of his childhood. Ella made his day brighter just by being there. She made him feel better.

And that scared him as much as it reassured him. Ella was special. He really ought to walk away and let her find someone else—someone who deserved her. Someone who could give her his whole heart.

Yet he wasn't ready to let her go. Not yet. Which made him precisely the selfish, unlovable man that was in his genes. Precisely the wrong man for a woman who'd already been hurt by selfish, unlovable men—her absent father and her cheating fiancé.

And Rico didn't have a clue how he could make everything turn out right for both of them.

CHAPTER NINE

ELLA glanced at the screen and frowned. Rico didn't usually ring her during office hours. Was something wrong? 'Hello, Rico?'

'Ella *bellezza,* do you have your diary handy?'

'Yes. Why?'

'I need to book a meeting with you.'

'You're seeing me tonight,' she said. 'Why do you need to book a meeting with me?'

'Because the meeting's going to be about business and tonight's going to be about…' He laughed. 'Wait and see. Though benefits might be involved later.'

Warmth spread through her. 'What kind of business are we talking about?' she asked.

'A potential commission. A cake for a launch party in a month's time. So where do you want to meet? Your kitchen, or my office?'

She frowned again. 'Your office is in Rome.'

He coughed. 'My *London* office.'

Then the penny dropped. 'You bought the hotel?'

'Yup. We're re-launching The Fountain in four weeks. Is that enough notice for you to make me a cake?'

'Should be. Though we'll need to talk about size.'

He gave a rich chuckle that had her blushing.

'Rico!'

'You said it, not me, *bellezza*. OK. So you want to know how many guests I'm inviting and what kind of design I have in mind.'

'And what kind of flavours.' She paused. 'I can make a meeting any time after ten if it's here, and any time after about ten-thirty if it's at your office.'

'Let's make it four-thirty, today, at yours,' he said. 'And, Ella—this is official, by the way. It's a business deal, not a favour.'

'So you're getting quotes from elsewhere?' Some of the bubbles of pleasure burst.

'It's business,' he repeated. 'Though your prices are obviously market rate, and I already know the quality of your product. Give me the right design, and you get the commission. I'll email you the other details. See you at four-thirty. *Ciao, bellezza*.'

By the time Rico arrived, Ella had three pages full of sketches.

'Are those designs for me to approve?' he asked.

'Suggestions. Though I'll listen to what you have to say, first. They might be the complete opposite of what I've come up with.'

'You're the creative one,' Rico said. 'I'd rather see what you've been thinking about.'

'OK. First of all, I could do you a cake in the shape of the hotel. It'd be a scale model, of course.' She showed him the picture she'd sketched from the hotel's website.

'That's good,' he said.

'Or there's the fountain in the courtyard. I could do you a normal sheet cake, decorate it as a garden, and do you a sugar-paste replica of the fountain as a topper. If I use wires, I can do you droplets of water coming down from the fountain.' She showed him the sketches. 'Obviously this isn't *your* fountain. I'd have to come and take photo-

graphs of it so I could make an accurate sugar-paste replica. But it's an example of what I can do.'

'Impressive.'

She warmed to her theme. 'Or, if you'd rather the guests
had individual cakes rather than slices, I can make a tower
of cupcakes with a six-inch cake for cutting, like I do for
wedding cakes. And I could do you a smaller sugar-paste
fountain on top of the cutting cake.'

'I definitely want a fountain,' he said. 'Given the hotel's
name, I'm planning a chocolate fountain and a champagne
fountain, too.'

'So maybe the cupcakes would be best. It'd reflect the
shape of the other two fountains.'

He smiled. 'I like how your mind works. Price?'

She handed him a piece of paper without comment.

He scanned it swiftly. *Bene.* It's a deal.'

'I need to make the cupcakes on the day so they're
fresh,' she said, 'and then ice them. I take it you're doing
an evening launch?'

'Yes. And it'll be on a Saturday. Given that you've got
the café orders to do as well, that's going to be a lot of work
for you. Do you need me to send over one of my kitchen
staff to help you?'

'You wouldn't offer that to my competitors, would you?'
she asked.

'No.' He raised an eyebrow. 'But you're pulling out the
stops for me. And it's in my interest to make life easier for
you.' He leaned forward to steal a kiss. 'Think of it as…
extra benefits.'

The pictures he'd just put in her head made her cheeks
colour, and he laughed.

'So do you want to borrow staff?' he asked.

'Someone to do the café deliveries would save me some
time,' she admitted.

'I'll sort it.'

'What flavour do you want?'

He smiled. 'Guess.'

She rolled her eyes. 'Chocolate. If you've got a chocolate fountain as well, Rico, don't you think that'll be too much?'

'Is there such a thing as too much chocolate?' he asked.

She laughed. 'Now you sound like a girl.'

'Oh, do I?' He looked thoughtful. 'I might just have to make you take that back.'

He stood up, took her hand and yanked her into his arms. By the time he'd finished kissing her, Ella was completely breathless and dishevelled. 'OK. I admit. You're not girly in the slightest. You're all man,' she said. And how. She lifted her chin. 'But I thought this was supposed to be a business meeting?'

'It was. We've concluded our business. And we need to be elsewhere.'

'Do we?'

He produced two tickets from his pocket and handed them to her. The best seats in the house, at a performance where tickets were like gold dust. 'Wow. Rico, how did you…?'

'Let's just say there are some advantages to being a spoiled rich kid.' He stole a kiss. 'Go get your glad rags on, *bellezza*. Let's go and have some fun.'

Over the next couple of weeks, Rico and Ella fell into a habit of meeting up after work. Sometimes they went out; sometimes Rico turned up with a bag full of ingredients, which he stowed in Ella's fridge while he carried her off to bed, then cooked for her; and at the weekends they worked through their tour-guide list.

Ella couldn't remember ever being so happy. Neither of them had made a commitment to the future, but she was beginning to think that it'd be safe to trust Rico with her heart. Because maybe he was the man she'd thought he was, in Rome. Rico the CEO had a public face; she had the strongest feeling that Rico the tour guide was his private face, one he didn't show to just anybody.

On the Sunday morning, Rico rang Ella at six. 'Rise and shine, *bellezza*.'

'So much for my Sunday morning lie-in,' she grumbled. 'Why are we getting up so early?'

'Because today we're going somewhere not on our list. Oh, and you need your passport.'

'My passport?' Still half asleep, she couldn't get her head round the idea. 'Why?'

'Just bear with me on this—it's something I think you're going to like. I'll collect you in thirty minutes, OK?'

Bemused, she showered and dressed, and was ready when he rang her doorbell. When the taxi dropped them off at the airport, she frowned. 'Where are we going?'

'Through here. For breakfast.' Including superb Italian coffee.

'Where are we going?' she asked again, looking at the departure boards.

'That won't help you, *bellezza*. It's not a scheduled flight.'

She blinked. 'You're telling me you have a private plane?'

'No, it belongs to a friend.'

Her eyes narrowed. 'In the same way that your flat in Rome belonged to a friend?'

'No, it really belongs to a friend. Like the restaurant.' He spread his hands. 'Spoiled rich kid territory. Some of my friends have *great* toys. And we share.' He smiled. 'I'm lending Giuseppe my car for a month, in return.'

She laughed. 'Don't tell me—would this be an Italian sports car?'

'That predictable, am I?'

'Sure are,' she teased. 'Where are we going?'

He shrugged. 'About two and a half hours away.'

'Talk about vague! Rico…'

'Just go with it,' he said, and kissed her. 'It's somewhere I think you'll like. I know it's a bit decadent, nipping over to mainland Europe just for the day, but…wait and see.'

She didn't have a clue where they were going until they arrived at Vienna airport. And then she just gaped. 'I can't believe you're taking me to Vienna for the day.'

'You told me in Rome that you wanted to come here,' he said with a smile. 'I assume that's because of the cafés and the cakes.'

'Absolutely.' She could still barely believe he'd whisked her off here just for the day. 'Rico, this is the nicest thing anyone's ever done for me. Thank you.'

'My pleasure, *bellezza*.' He kissed her lightly.

They caught the train from the airport into the city, then changed to the underground and emerged onto the street near the cathedral, with its green and gold chevrons on the roof. 'Wow, what gorgeous architecture,' she said. 'Vienna's beautiful.' The wide, wide street was flanked with five-storey white and pastel-coloured buildings, and she'd never seen so many windows.

'Come on. There's somewhere we need to be.'

'Where?'

'You'll see when we get there.'

Rico had clearly put a lot of thought and planning into this, and Ella was intrigued rather than annoyed by his vagueness.

He took her to one of the oldest *Konditoreien* in Vienna; she was enthralled by the glass cabinet displaying what looked like fifty different types of cake, as well as displays of confectionery.

'Come on. The café's upstairs.' He led her through to the stairs at the back of the shop.

'Wow, look at that chandelier,' she said as they reached the top of the stairs. 'That's beautiful. And this whole place—it's like being transported back into a much more glamorous age.'

'I'm glad you like it.' And he was relieved that it lived up to the pictures he'd seen on the website. 'Apparently the classic coffee here is a melange,' he said, pronouncing the word *mel-anj,* as if it were French rather than German. 'And I think we should have cake to go with it.'

'How on earth do you choose from a selection as tempting as that?' Ella asked, staring at the display. 'Though I guess, as we're in Vienna, I ought to choose Sachertorte.'

He kissed the spot just behind her ear. 'We're going to Café Sacher for that, a bit later. So you can try something else.'

Eventually she chose the Esterhazytorte. 'I love layered cakes,' she said as they went back to their seats. 'We had an Aussie temp at the accountancy firm, and she introduced me to hummingbird cake.'

'Obviously it's not made from hummingbirds, so what is it really?'

'Kind of like carrot cake, but made with tropical fruit. Banana and pineapple, normally, but I've got a recipe for a version that includes mango and passion fruit.' She looked at him. 'You'd really like it. If you're good, I might make you one.'

He leaned closer. 'Good at what?' he whispered in her ear.

She blushed spectacularly, and he laughed. 'Ah, *bellezza.* You're so easy to tease.'

The waitress came with their coffees, two small glasses of water, and two slices of cake.

'Oh, I really like this—it's kind of a cross between a latte and cappuccino but without the icky cocoa on top,' Ella said when she'd tried the coffee.

'I thought you liked chocolate?'

'Not quite as much as you do, and definitely not on my coffee.' She smiled at him and tried the cake. 'This is lush. Almond sponge and hazelnut cream. Try it.' She fed him from her fork.

'Very nice.' He waited until they'd finished their coffee. 'Ready for the next bit?'

'Next?'

The look on her face when they went through a side door and were met by the head pastry chef with white coats and hats, and she realised he'd arranged a tour of the kitchens for her, was priceless.

The worktops were all marble; one pastry chef was working on flat-icing a line of chocolate cakes, while others were mixing batters, making frosting or laying out the delicate pastry for making apple strudel.

But the standout for Ella was a sheet cake with a beautiful Lipizzaner horse on top, which a pastry chef was delicately painting. 'That's stunning. Look at the sugar-paste work on his ears, and the saddle.'

The pastry chef talked her through various painting techniques. Rico wasn't that interested in the details, but he loved seeing the expression on Ella's face. She was clearly taking it all in, asking questions to clarify points here and there.

Yep, he'd definitely planned the perfect day for her. And it was true what he'd told her: in pleasing her, he was giving himself real pleasure. He'd never felt like that before.

'That was amazing,' she said when they left. 'I can't believe you did that for me. Thank you. That was so special.'

'I'm glad you liked it.' He loved her enthusiasm. And it was definitely catching. 'We're right next door to the Hofburg Palace. Do you fancy playing tourist?'

She nodded, beaming. 'I'd love to.'

They wandered hand in hand through the imperial apartments, listening to the commentary from the audio guide.

'Ankle-length hair. I'm not sure I could cope with that,' Ella said. 'Three hours every morning just to have your hair dressed. It'd drive me crazy!'

But she paused in front of a portrait of Empress Sisi in a white dress. 'Wow. She really was beautiful.'

There was a case by the portrait, displaying reproductions of the diamond stars the empress wore in her hair. 'You'd look lovely with those in your hair,' Rico said.

She shook her head. 'My hair's not really long enough. And you'd need dark hair to set them off properly.' She paused. 'They'd look very nice done in icing.'

He blinked. 'You could make them in icing?'

'Sure. I'd use a glacé icing rather than buttercream. And then I'd do the stars separately, in fondant. If you paint white icing with a mix of silver lustre dust and alcohol, it'll look silver. And then you can use white glimmer sugar for the diamonds.'

'Glimmer sugar?'

'The sparkly sprinkles I use on cakes.'

He laughed. 'I love the way you see everything in terms of cake.'

'Well, hey, Vienna's practically the capital of the cake world,' she teased back. 'And you know the saying. When in Vienna…'

He gave her a speaking look. 'It's "when in Rome".'

She grinned. 'It works for Vienna, too.'

They lingered in the gift-shop, and Rico noticed that she looked closely at a replica of the Sisi star. Interesting. But he also noticed that she didn't buy it.

When they'd left the palace, they wandered through the city centre, window-shopping. Rico still couldn't get the diamond stars out of his head. 'You don't wear much jewellery, do you?' He glanced at her. 'Just a watch. And your ears aren't pierced.'

'I'm too chicken to have my ears pierced, and clip-on earrings just aren't comfortable. I do sometimes wear a necklace, but jewellery just gets in the way when I'm working.'

A necklace. He spotted a replica of the Sisi star, made into a choker, in one of the seriously expensive jewellery shops. Something like the one in the palace gift shop, only using real gemstones rather than being costume jewellery. He could just imagine Ella wearing nothing but the choker, and his temperature spiked.

'Time for Sachertorte, I think,' he said, and took her to the famous café. 'Excuse me for a second?' he said after they'd ordered.

'Sure.'

With any luck, she'd think he'd gone to the loo and there was a queue. Making sure she didn't see him leave the café, he made a swift exit, returned to the jeweller's and bought the star choker. He stowed the box in his pocket, where she wouldn't notice it, and came back to join her, all smiles.

'I was beginning to wonder if you'd got lost,' she said. 'Your coffee must be almost cold by now.'

'Which is how Italians drink their coffee anyway,' he reminded her, and promptly downed his espresso in one.

As they walked back through the streets she insisted on stopping at one of the chocolate shops. 'Ju's almost as much of a chocolate fiend as you are. I'd like to bring something back for her.'

He looked in the window. 'It says here that this used to be one of the imperial court confectioners, so they must be good.'

'Give me two minutes.'

He knew from Rome that she wasn't one for dragging round the shops, and was happy to browse through the displays while she picked what she wanted.

He held her hand all the way home to London. Back at her flat, she handed him a bag from the confectioner's they'd browsed in.

'For me? I thought you were buying chocolate for Julia?'

'I did. But I bought some for you, too. I know you love the stuff.' She shrugged. 'It's not much. Just a token, really. But I wanted to say thank you, and let you know I appreciate how much you spoiled me today.'

'*Bellezza,* you didn't have to give me anything. But thank you.' It touched him that she'd thought of him. And she'd bought him a gift that he really appreciated, the tiny Lilliput chocolates that were a speciality of the confectioner's. None of his exes would've done that; he was more used to being taken for granted.

'Since you've just given me a present—I have one for you, too.' He took the box from his pocket and handed it to her.

Ella stared at the beautifully wrapped box, and her heart skipped a beat for a moment. It was clearly from a jeweller's. But of course it wouldn't be a ring. Neither of them had said how they felt about each other; and anyway the box was too big.

She undid the ribbon and opened the box to see a beautiful silver star, a replica of the ones that the empress had worn in her hair; it was a choker on a black chiffon ribbon. She'd almost bought one of these in the gift shop, and with Rico being so observant he'd clearly noticed. And he'd remembered that she didn't wear bracelets or a watch for work. He'd bought her the perfect piece of jewellery. She had absolutely no idea when he'd managed to buy it, but she was thrilled that he'd bought her something so beautiful.

'Thank you. It's gorgeous.' She kissed him.

And this was definitely a kind of declaration from him. A ring was out of the question as it was too symbolic; but she knew he was telling her that, for him, she was as beautiful as that long-ago empress. And maybe, just maybe, he was telling her that he was ready to start opening up to her. Letting her close. Making this more than just being acquaintances with benefits.

'It's been the perfect day.' She held him closer. 'And I'm not ready for it to end, yet. Will you stay tonight, Rico?'

Stay.

He never stayed the night with anyone. It meant letting someone too close. He'd been tempted several times to break his rule for Ella, but he'd held himself back. Just. Though he, too, wasn't ready for the day to end just yet. And one night wouldn't hurt, would it?

'And your alarm goes off when, exactly?' he asked, feigning a coolness he definitely didn't feel.

She grimaced. 'Half-past five. Sorry.'

He smiled. 'I'm not usually up *quite* that early but, for you… Yes.' He kissed her. 'I'll stay.'

CHAPTER TEN

LATER in the week, on impulse, Ella texted Rico. *Taste-tester required.*

It took a while for him to reply, but he eventually came back with, *Happy to interview. Where and when?*

She smiled. *My kitchen, when you've finished today. Arrive hungry.*

And she knew full well he'd have more than one interpretation for that.

Her phone beeped at six. *On way. **Starving**.*

By the time Rico knocked on the door, the cakes were cooled and iced.

He kissed her hello. 'Something smells gorgeous.'

'I hope you're hungry.'

'Very.' He kissed her again, this time more lingeringly.

'Take a seat.' She set three cupcakes before him, a bowl of lemon sorbet and a glass of iced water.

'What's this for?' he asked, indicating the sorbet.

'Cleansing your palate, so you can distinguish between the flavours properly.'

He took a bite of the first one. 'Mmm. That's gorgeous. And the cake's different.'

'The base is hummingbird cake rather than vanilla,' she told him.

He smiled. 'You said in Vienna that you'd make me a hummingbird cake if I was good.'

'And I will, if you are,' she said, smiling back. 'What about the icing?'

He thought for a moment. 'Orange. Yes, it works.'

'It should do, because that's the traditional cream cheese frosting that goes with the cake. Eat some lemon sorbet, now.'

He looked pained. 'Don't I get to eat the rest of the cake? Especially as it's only a small one?'

'Later. You're taste-testing, first.'

He ate a spoonful of the sorbet, then sipped the water. 'OK. Cake two.' He took a bite. 'I like this one more. That's lime in the topping, isn't it? There's more of a zing than the orange one.'

She made a note. 'OK. Third one?'

After more sorbet and more water, he tried the third. 'No. Too sweet.'

'That's vanilla buttercream. I thought it might be wrong with the cake. But I wanted a taste-tester's opinion.' She smiled at him. 'From someone I happen to know is a real foodie and would be honest with me.'

'It needs a proper zing. My vote's for the second, the lime one.'

'Noted. Now I know what I'm doing.'

He looked at her. 'So that was it? Just three?'

'Well, I didn't want to overwhelm you with flavours.'

He looked disappointed. 'And there was I, thinking I had a whole plateful of cakes to try. Like the ones with the pretty icing you did for your launch.'

'The two-tone ones, you mean?'

'Though I guess they're complicated.'

'On the contrary. They're dead easy.' She smiled at him. 'Give me a few minutes, and you can ice your own.'

'You're kidding.'

'It only takes five minutes to whip up a batch of cup-cakes. But you're going to get messy,' she warned. She looked at him. 'That white shirt has to go.'

'What?'

'That white shirt has to go,' she repeated. 'Especially if we're doing coloured icing. I'm not sure your laundry service would be able to get the colour out.'

'So what does that make me, the Naked Baker?' he asked, laughing.

She laughed back. 'Semi. And you can have an apron, if you want.'

'An apron?' He gave her a disgusted look. 'I don't think so.' He took his shirt off. 'Where do I put this?'

'I'll deal with it.' She hung it up out of the way, and smiled. 'Mmm. Nice pecs, Signor Rossi.'

'You could take your shirt off, too,' he said, looking hopeful.

'Ha, you wish. But we're making cake.'

Five minutes later, she had the ingredients and a set of scales on the worktop in front of him, and had him mixing up the batter for the cupcakes and then spooning it into cake cases.

He looked at her and smiled. 'This is actually quite fun. I can see why you enjoy it. So what do we do while the cakes are cooking?' he asked as she put the cakes in the oven.

'Trust you to be thinking two steps ahead. We make the icing.'

'And there was I, thinking we'd have time out.'

'Not unless you want the cakes to burn. Focus, man, *focus*.'

He laughed. 'You're so bossy, Ella.'

'Says you,' she shot back, but she was laughing as well.

She talked him through making the icing, step by step, and took the cakes out of the oven to cool. Then she handed him a paintbrush.

'What's this for?'

'I'm teaching you my secret. Two-tone icing is the easiest thing in the world.'

She dropped a nozzle with a rounded star tip into a disposable icing bag, and took the top off the pot of one of the coloured icing pastes she used.

'That looks like ink,' he said, peering at it.

'You're not far off, but it's edible. What you do now is dip the brush in, and draw a line inside the bag. Don't get it on your hands.'

He frowned. 'I thought you said it was edible?'

'It is, but if you really want to explain to your colleagues why your hands are bright purple tomorrow morning...'

'Got it.'

'Now spread the line with the paintbrush. Any way you like.'

He looked speculatively at the brush, then at her. 'Now, if this was melted chocolate...'

What he was thinking was, oh, so obvious. She laughed. 'This is a professional kitchen, Rico. No painting of body parts. It's against all the hygiene regulations, and you know it.'

'Spoilsport,' he said. 'I'm very tempted to try and change your mind.'

And it wouldn't take much for him to do it. She sucked in a breath and willed herself to stay professional. 'I'm teaching you to do the icing—on your request. So pay attention.'

He gave her an insolent salute. *'Sì, signorina.'*

'Now press the bag together so the colour's spread evenly.'

He did so, then lifted it up and inspected it. 'It doesn't look as if there's any colour in there.'

'There's enough. You'll see in a moment.' She took the brush from him, then spooned the buttercream into the bag.

'I see it now,' he said, as the rich, deep purple spread against the ivory-coloured buttercream.

'And now,' she said, 'you simply pipe out the icing until the colour starts to show on the edges.' She demonstrated. '*Voilà*, two-tone icing. And then all you do is start in the middle of the cake and pipe a spiral, slightly overlapping the icing as you go.' She handed him the bag, then fetched one of the cakes and set it on a plate. 'Go for it.'

He tried. 'Nothing's coming out of the bag.'

'Because you're not holding the bag right—you need to grip it between your forefinger and thumb.'

'I am.'

She came to stand behind him, and moved his hands. 'Try now. Push downwards, keeping your finger and thumb jammed flat together so the icing can't escape through it.'

'Problem,' he said.

'What?'

He turned round to face her. 'You just took a step back. It was much nicer when you had your arms round me.'

'I'm going to get in your way when you're icing the cake.'

'No, you're not.' He gave her a speculative look. 'And, as I said earlier, you could lose your shirt. You, me, and nothing in between.'

Oh, the pictures that put in her head. Skin to skin with Rico. '*Not* in my kitchen.' Though it was a real effort not to follow through on his suggestion; right now she was seriously aroused. If he touched her, she'd be lost. And she had to sit on her own hands to stop herself touching him.

He proceeded to pipe a perfect spiral on the cake.

She blinked. 'Either you've done this before, or you're a natural.'

He looked at her. 'I know that movement.' He moistened his lower lip with the tip of his tongue. 'Only not on a cake.'

She frowned. 'I'm not with you.'

He gave her a wolfish smile. 'Then let me demonstrate, *bellezza*.' He put the icing bag down. Before she realised what he was going to do, he'd hiked her skirt up, his hand was inside her knickers, and his thumb was working in a spiral on her clitoris.

'Oh-h-h.' The word was a moan of pure pleasure.

'You're wet for me, *bellezza*,' he murmured.

'Yes,' she admitted, her voice husky.

'Let me take your shirt off now,' he said softly. 'And I don't give a damn about hygiene regulations. I want you. Right here, right now.' His thumb moved again, sending another wave of pleasure through her.

Part of her really wanted to go with this.

But.

'Rico, the blind's up,' she whispered.

He stopped as her words registered. 'So anyone could see in.'

'Uh-huh. And while you being topless isn't a problem, me being topless—or people working out where your hand is right now...' She bit her lip.

'Close your eyes, *bellezza*.'

She did so, and felt coolness against her skin as he moved away from her. Then she heard the sound of the blind being wound down.

'Problem solved,' he said softly, and jammed his mouth over hers. The next thing she knew, he'd lifted her onto the worktop—still kissing her—and her skirt was right up round her waist. A couple of seconds later, he'd removed her shirt and her bra, and his body was easing into hers.

She forgot completely about hygiene regulations and rules. All she could focus on was the way Rico made her feel, the way he took her closer and closer to the edge, setting up a hard and fast rhythm that had her pulse racing to meet it.

He smeared cool icing across her nipple, making her gasp—and then followed it up by sucking the sugary confection from her skin, making her gasp even more as his teeth grazed her skin.

And then her body slammed into climax and she held onto him for dear life, feeling him shudder against her as he reached his own climax.

What had just happened was unbelievable. And Ella knew that she was going to be thinking about this evening every time she iced cupcakes from now on.

Rico helped her clear up downstairs, then demolished most of the mini hummingbird cakes. 'I'll see you tomorrow, *bellezza,*' he said softly. 'Sweet dreams.'

'You, too.' She kissed him goodbye.

As he went back to the hotel Rico really wished that he'd stayed over tonight. So he could wake up in her arms again, even if it was going to be at an unearthly hour.

Which was crazy. It meant he wanted to get involved with her. Seriously involved. The idea terrified him and drew him in equal measure. What did he know of love? And no way did he want to make himself vulnerable.

Though maybe, just maybe, Ella was the one he could trust with himself.

CHAPTER ELEVEN

'SATURDAY,' Rico said. 'The launch party.'

Ella nodded. 'Everything's on schedule as far as I'm concerned. The topper's almost done—and no, you can't see it until the day. No previews allowed. You just have to trust me with it, OK?'

'Of course I trust you.' He smiled. 'Anyway, I wasn't thinking about that, *bellezza*. I was merely checking that you're coming as my guest.'

She frowned. 'Well, I'll be a bit busy, sorting out the cake.'

'That won't take all night, and I want you there with me.'

She wrinkled her nose. 'Rico, I'd be happier in the background. I don't really fit into your world.'

He flapped his hand dismissively. 'Sure you do.'

'How? You own a chain of glamorous boutique hotels. I make cakes.'

'You make *fabulous* cakes,' he corrected. 'And, excuse me, who is it who always tells me that it's not how much money you have, it's how you treat other people that matters? You're good with people. And I want you with me.'

Put like that, how could she refuse? 'OK. Though I don't have anything suitable to wear to a launch party. And I really don't have the time right now for clothes-shopping.' She sighed. 'I guess I'll just have to make the time.'

He drew her close. 'Could you shop online, get stuff delivered to you and try them on when it suits you? Then you wouldn't have to drag round the shops.'

'Then I'll have to wait in for the courier,' she grumbled. 'And if they turn up when I'm out on a delivery, it'll be the next day before they can re-deliver, or I'll have to trek over to their warehouse to pick it up.'

'Get everything delivered to the hotel, and I'll ask my PA here to return the things you don't like.' He paused. 'Or tell me the kind of thing you want and I'll ask her to call the designers and get them to send in a selection of dresses.'

'My own private fashion show, you mean?' She shook her head. 'It's very sweet of you to think of that, but you know what I think about designer clothes. They're over-priced and they only suit one body type. Which isn't mine.'

'I happen to like your body type, so don't even think about changing it.' He moulded her curves with his hands. 'Or turning into one of those boring women who count every single calorie and every single carb.'

That made her smile. 'Hardly, doing what I do for a living.'

He stroked her face. 'Would you let me buy the dress for you, *bellezza*?'

She folded her arms. 'Thank you for the offer, but I can buy my own dress.'

'I know you can, *bellezza*. I'm trying to do something nice for you, not be a control freak.' He gave her a rueful smile. 'It's my fault that you have to go clothes-shopping, so I'm trying to minimise the time impact for you.'

She leaned her forehead against his. 'And I'm being an ungrateful cow. Sorry. It must be the wrong time of the month.'

'No, you're just really busy at the moment and I'm making demands on time you don't have. But I do want you at the party with me, Ella *bellezza*.'

'I'll be there. Is your family coming to the launch?' she asked.

'No. My grandparents are too frail to travel.'

Yet again, she noticed, he didn't mention his parents. And she was curious—why was Rico estranged from them? She still hadn't persuaded him to open up to her about his family, even though she'd told him all about her own difficult background.

Before she could ask anything else, he switched the subject back to her clothes. But she noticed. And she wondered.

Rico was busy keeping the Italian side of his business ticking over on the phone and by email while the English side was coming together; the time he could spend with Ella before the launch was severely limited, and it put him out of sorts. With her, he felt grounded. And when he realised that, it put him out of sorts even more. He didn't want to rely on someone else for his happiness, even if that person was as sweet-natured as Ella.

The day of the launch dawned, and the whole hotel was busy preparing for it while minimising the disruption to their guests. Rico barely had time to speak to Ella during the day, apart from kissing her hello, giving her a key to his suite so she could change into her dress for the party, and telling her to see the chef if there was anything she needed from the kitchen.

Though he did see the cake just as she added the finishing touches.

Ella had made him a pyramid of cupcakes swirled with alternate white and dark chocolate ganache; at the top was a white chocolate iced cutting cake with tall curls of chocolate standing round the outside, topped with a sugar-paste fountain, with droplets of water coming down on almost invisible wires.

'Ella *bellezza,* that looks amazing,' he said.

'You really do like it? You're not just being polite?' she asked.

'I'm not being polite,' he reassured her. 'It's perfect.' He kissed her. 'Thank you.'

Once the party started, Rico had interviews to give and journalists and photographers to show round. He noted how many photographs were taken of the cake; Ella would definitely get some good publicity from this. Which she deserved—she'd worked hard to make sure the cake was perfect for tonight.

After the journalists, there were the movers and shakers, people who could use their conference and event facilities, and Rico went into full sales mode.

But best of all was when everyone had gone home. Everyone except Ella, dressed in a very plain black dress and high heels, with the glittering star he'd bought her in Vienna at her throat and her hair pinned in a swish updo. Desire kicked through him. He'd never seen her look more beautiful.

'I never got to dance with you tonight,' he said.

She smiled. 'That's OK.'

'No, it isn't. And I've neglected you all evening.'

'Because you were working and you had a lot of people you needed to talk to.' She stroked his face. 'It really is OK, Rico. I understand.'

He was so used to demands from his previous girlfriends that the lack of them from Ella floored him slightly. 'Everyone loved the cake. The picture might end up in a few colour supplements—and on the Internet,' he said.

'Good. Just make sure there's a picture of it on your hotel website with a link to mine,' she said with a grin.

He grinned back. 'It sounds like you're building an empire, Ella *bellezza*.'

'Maybe. Right now,' she said, 'I'm really, really happy. Life doesn't get any better than this.'

'You know what? I was thinking just the same. But, actually, it does get better.'

She frowned. 'How?'

'I'm kidnapping you.' He scooped her up and strode over to the lift.

She laughed. 'Rico, are you taking me to your suite?'

'Better than that.'

He set her on her feet once they were inside the lift, and made sure her body was in full contact with his all the way down, so she was left in no doubt about his arousal. Once the doors had closed, he kissed her until they were both breathless; the lift doors had opened and closed several times before he realised that they were on the floor he wanted.

'This isn't the way to your suite—or did you move after I got changed?' she asked.

'This is just for tonight.' He opened the door to the honeymoon suite.

Just as he'd planned, there was a bottle of good champagne on ice. He plugged his MP3 player into a dock, and a smoky-voiced jazz artist started singing a love song to the accompaniment of a piano and double-bass. Then he turned the lights down low.

'Dance with me, Ella *bellezza*?' he said.

Oh, wow. Today had been a big deal for him, she knew. The launch of his first hotel in London—his first hotel outside Italy. He'd been busy with the launch party for weeks, talking to journalists and potential clients, making sure he got the right attention for the business.

She'd stayed in the background tonight, knowing that his work needed to come first and not wanting to be in the way. And she'd watched him, proud of the way he didn't let a single question put him off his stride. He knew everything about the hotel and its staff; he hadn't had to ask anyone else to clarify a single thing for him.

And yet, despite everything that had been going on, he'd still planned these quiet moments just for them. She had no idea when he'd found the time to think about it, let alone organise it, but it touched her to the heart.

She smiled. 'I'd love to dance with you, Rico.'

And there, in his arms, dancing with him, it hit her. *She'd fallen for him.*

She couldn't pinpoint the exact moment when, but she loved him. She loved his strength, she loved his sense of humour, and she loved the way he could switch from hard-headed businessman to intensely focused lover. She loved the way he noticed things but didn't make a fuss about them. And the quiet way he dealt with things had taught her that she could trust him. He didn't make promises unless he knew he could keep them. Since Rome, he'd been scrupulously honest with her.

And she was sure that he was finally letting her closer. OK, so he hadn't made any kind of declaration, and she had a feeling that Rico would rather stick pins in his eyes than talk about emotions—but that didn't mean he didn't feel them.

She wasn't going to tell him how she felt about him in words—she didn't want him to back off—but she could tell him with her body.

This time, when he kissed her, there was no holding

back—within seconds the kiss turned deep and demanding and hot.

And actually, no, she wasn't going to hold back the words. She'd just have to say them in a way she knew he'd accept. 'Rico,' she whispered, 'I want you.'

'I want you, too,' he whispered back.

And she had the strongest feeling that they meant the same thing by 'want'.

Rico unzipped her little black dress, slowly eased it down so she could step out of it, then hung it carefully over the back of the sofa. The diamond star at her throat glittered; he still hadn't got round to telling her that it was diamond and white gold, not silver and cubic zircona. And he really hoped she wouldn't consider it a lie when he finally confessed. OK, so he hadn't corrected her assumption that it was costume jewellery; but that was a little bit of misdirection rather than an out-and-out lie, so he could spoil her without her feeling bad about it.

He gently removed the choker and kissed his way along her throat. 'Your skin's so soft.' And her perfume was light and enticing, making him want more.

Her underwear was lacy, the black in sharp contrast to her ivory skin. He hooked his fingers under the straps of her bra and drew them down to bare her shoulders. 'You're lush, Ella *bellezza*,' he said, his voice low. 'Absolutely lush. You make me ache for you.'

In answer, she kissed him hard.

He undid the pins in her hair and let it fall down. *'Bellezza.'* His voice cracked with desire; he picked her up, carried her through to the bedroom, and lay her down on the four-poster bed.

'I think you're a little overdressed, Rico,' she said with a smile.

He considered stripping for her, but he knew that right now he didn't have the patience to have any kind of finesse. Instead, he stripped in ten seconds flat, then finished removing her clothes.

'What happened to seduction?' she asked, laughing.

'I just can't wait any more. I need you now.' He paused only long enough to grab a condom to protect her. And then at last he was where he wanted to be, inside her, her body tightening round him, warm and wet and welcoming. He pushed deeper; she sighed with pleasure and slid her hands into his hair, drawing his head down to hers and then kissing him, demanding and giving all at the same time.

This was what he'd needed all day. His Ella.

Her body tightened round his, tipping him into his own climax. He held her tightly, wanting this moment to last for ever.

Though of course it couldn't. He went to the bathroom, then came back to lie beside her.

'It's Saturday night. Stay with me tonight?' he asked. 'I'll drive you home tomorrow, or if you give me your key I'll drive over first thing in the morning and pick up a change of clothes for you.'

She smiled. 'Yes.'

'I forgot the champagne. I guess I rushed you a bit.' He kissed her. 'Sorry.'

'Nothing to apologise for. I wasn't saying no.'

'I guess. Stay there.' He went to fetch the champagne and glasses.

'That's so decadent, drinking champagne in bed,' she said, accepting a glass from him. 'Mmm, and this is nice stuff.'

'Glad you like it, Ella *bellezza*.'

'And I like this room. A proper four-poster.'

'And there's a whirlpool bath in the bathroom.' He eyed

her speculatively. 'Which I think would go very well with the champagne.'

She rolled her eyes. 'The Roman boy goes in search of yet another fountain.' But she let him lead her into the bathroom. And he thoroughly enjoyed taking a whirlpool bath with her, teasing her and arousing her until she climaxed again under his touch.

Later that night, Rico lay awake. He never asked his girlfriends to stay over. If anything, he made sure they didn't get that close and he kept them away from his private domain. But having Ella beside him—he couldn't even begin to explain to himself how it made him feel. All he knew was that he wanted this. And he wanted more.

And it scared the hell out of him.

She'd been hurt before. What if he let her down? He'd promised her that he wouldn't let her down...and he didn't intend to. But what if he failed? He hadn't been enough for his parents to love him. And he knew that his grandparents had seen him as the heir to the hotel empire rather than for himself. Could he be something more than that, for Ella?

In business, he never doubted his judgement. Emotionally, it was a whole different ballgame. And one where he didn't have a clue what the rules were.

Waking with her in his arms was definitely something Rico wanted to do again. It made the whole morning feel full of sunshine.

'Well, Signor Hotel Tycoon, what are the plans for today?' she asked.

'Whatever you want to do. I'm in your hands.'

She gave him a truly sensual smile. 'Good. I have an idea...'

An idea that blew his mind and put a smile on his face.

And, after he'd driven Ella home to change, Rico enjoyed walking along the river with her again.

'So now The Fountain is relaunched, does this mean you're going back to Rome?' she asked.

'Not yet. I'm spending the next week doing a few hours in every role, so I can work out what the staff training needs are.'

She gave him a speculative look. 'You're going to be a waiter, then?'

'Yes.'

'I'm so tempted to come and pester you and be a difficult client.'

He just laughed. 'You can try. I'm good with difficult clients.'

'Hmm. That sounds like a challenge. When exactly are you on duty?'

'Tuesday morning. Ready for morning coffee at ten o'clock.'

She grinned. 'Oh, this is going to be *such* fun.'

On Tuesday morning, Ella dropped off the orders at the cafés, then headed for Rico's hotel.

'Good morning, madam. May I show you to a table?' Rico asked.

He was dressed the same as the other waiters, in a fitted burgundy jacket, white shirt and black trousers. And he looked utterly delectable. She smiled at him. 'Thank you. May I have a table with a view of the garden?'

'Of course, madam.' He ushered her to a table, held the chair out for her, then brought her a menu.

When he came back to take her order, Ella purred, 'What do you recommend?'

He gave her a sultry look. 'That depends whether

madam is in the mood for light and frothy, or dark and intense.'

She burst out laughing. 'Rico, you're a terrible waiter. I hope you don't say that sort of thing to all your clients.'

He grinned and took a seat opposite her. 'Only to you. What I recommend for you, madam, isn't actually on the menu.'

She went hot at the thought.

'But, if I'm recommending something to you as a customer, then I think you'd like the cappuccino here. And, yes, I'll ask them to hold the cocoa dusting because I know you hate it.'

'Sounds good to me. Anything else?'

He went back into official waiter mode. 'All the cakes are fresh today, madam, if you'd like to make a selection from the counter.'

'Is your counter as good as the one we went to in Vienna?'

He gave her a speaking look. 'The Fountain Hotel isn't a specialist patisserie, madam. But I believe we are looking at a new supplier. The hotel owner has made a recommendation to the head chef.' He glanced at his watch. 'Who might have time for a word with her right now, if madam isn't busy.'

She smiled. 'I only came to test your waiting skills, Rico.'

He grinned. 'I believe in multi-tasking. Seriously. I told John about the hummingbird cakes, and he says he'd like samples.'

'Then I'll make a proper appointment and bring samples with me,' she said.

'Hmm. I might have to work a shift in the kitchen, that day.'

'Behave. And I must tell the head waiter that his staff

leaves a lot to be desired. I ordered a cup of coffee about half an hour ago and my waiter still hasn't brought it.' She tapped her watch.

'It wasn't anywhere near half an hour ago. And *you're* the one who wanted to talk.' He rolled his eyes. 'All right. Hint taken. I'll go and get your coffee, *bellezza*.'

When he came back, he had other customers to attend to; Ella watched him, and he was thoroughly charming, smiling and paying attention to what his guests wanted. The four middle-aged women he served would definitely be repeating their visit, she thought. He'd made all of them smile and feel special.

Though not *quite* as special as the way he made her feel.

Then she took a sip of the coffee.

It was absolutely vile.

She blew out a breath. She knew Rico would want to know the truth, but she'd have to find a nice way of telling him.

He came back over to her table. 'Is everything OK, *bellezza?* You've barely touched your coffee.'

She bit her lip. 'Rico, I'm so sorry. It's just, um, not how I'd normally have a cappuccino.'

'You mean it tastes revolting?' He frowned. 'That's not good. I apologise on behalf of the kitchen, and obviously I need to keep an eye on quality control. Or maybe change the coffee machine they use at the moment. May I?' He tasted it, then looked at her in surprise. 'Ella, it tastes fine to me.'

'Maybe it's me.' She shrugged. 'I'm probably overtired and I've drunk too much coffee lately,' she said.

'Let me get you something else.' He came back with a peppermint tea.

It was really refreshing, and the first sip took away the slight queasiness the coffee had induced. 'That's lovely.

Thank you.' She paused. 'Would you do that for all your customers?'

'Yes. You don't think you're getting special treatment just because you happen to be dating the owner, do you?'

She laughed. 'Well, am I?'

'Well, I wouldn't actually taste anyone else's coffee,' he admitted, 'and I wouldn't be sitting here opposite them, chatting. But I would make sure that anything they weren't happy with was replaced.' He sighed. 'You're a distraction, *bellezza*.'

'Go and do your work, *garçon*,' she teased.

He leaned over to steal a kiss. '*Garçon*, indeed. I'll see you later. And I meant it about ringing John. I want those hummingbird cakes on the menu.'

'Yes, sir.' She gave him a teasing salute. 'Can I pay my bill?'

'No. Because it's on me,' he said. '*Ciao, bellezza*.'

Later that evening, lying on the sofa with Rico, Ella stroked his hair back from his forehead. 'Sorry I put you off, this morning.'

'Actually, I quite liked having you around. Though I did have to explain to the other ladies I was serving that I was actually the owner of the hotel doing a bit of quality control work, and you were my girlfriend—my staff didn't really go around kissing random customers.'

She laughed. 'Were they very disappointed?'

He laughed back. 'Oh, you're such a bad girl.'

'So are you happy with the way things are going at The Fountain?' she asked.

'Yes. I have a good team. Some of the management needs replacing, but I'll handle that myself until I get the right person to do it.'

'So you're staying in London for a bit longer?'

'Yes.' But wild horses wouldn't drag it from him that the real reason he was staying was Ella. He could quite easily send a manager from one of his other hotels to take over in London, but right now he wanted to be in London. With her. And if he had to make up excuses to do it, so be it.

CHAPTER TWELVE

'IT's officially lunchtime, but obviously you're working through your lunch break today,' Rico said.

'No, I'm having a proper break. See?' Ella gestured to her plate and glass.

Rico eyed her sandwich and grimaced. 'That doesn't look very nice, Ella *bellezza*.'

'Actually, it's gorgeous.'

'What is it?'

She smiled. 'Marmite and celery.'

He looked completely baffled. 'Marmite?'

'It's an English thing, a yeast-extract spread,' she explained. 'Very savoury. People either love it or hate it. Try a bite.' She gestured to the plate.

He did as she suggested, and then had to take a gulp of her orange juice to take the taste away. 'Ella, how can you possibly eat that? It's repulsive!'

She shrugged. 'As I said, people either love it or hate it. I'm on the pro side.'

He pulled a face. 'I'll believe you. Otherwise I'd say it'd have to be a food craving.'

She rolled her eyes. 'I'm not pregnant, Rico.' Then she went white.

He felt his eyes narrow. 'What's wrong, *bellezza*?'

She lifted one hand, gesturing to him to wait; she was

clearly running through something in her head. 'Oh.' She bit her lip.

'What?'

'I'm late.' She took a breath. 'Two weeks late.'

Rico went cold. 'Is that normal for you?'

She bit her lip again and shook her head. 'Though it's probably just because I've been working madly. Last time I worked this hard, my periods went all over the place. And we've been careful.'

But the only one hundred per cent guaranteed contraception was abstinence. And he knew she knew it, too. 'Ella, you need to do a test.'

'You're overreacting.'

He stared at her in disbelief. 'Your period's two weeks late, you say that's not normal for you, and you tell me I'm *overreacting*?'

'I don't have any other symptoms of being pregnant.'

'Yes, you do.' Memories slid into his head. 'The other day, you didn't like the coffee and it tasted perfectly normal to me. And you're tired all the time.'

'Because I've been working hard. You're probably right about burnout. And I haven't been feeling sick or anything like that.'

Oh, man, was she in denial. It was all adding up for him. Nastily so. 'Not everyone feels sick. My best friend's wife didn't. You need to do a pregnancy test,' he repeated.

'It's not the kind of thing I have just lying around my bathroom, you know.' She narrowed her eyes at him.

'Fine. I'll go and buy one. Is there a pharmacy near here?'

'I don't need to do a pregnancy test,' she repeated. 'I'm fine.'

He folded his arms. 'Where's the pharmacy?'

'Don't bully me, Rico.'

'I'm not bullying you.' Though he was having a hard time containing his irritation. She was being ridiculously stubborn about something that would take only minutes to sort out. If the test was negative, they could both start breathing again and go back to normal. If it was positive...

He didn't even want to think about that right now. 'OK, if you're not going to tell me, let's do it the quick way.' He grabbed his mobile phone, flicked into the Internet and tapped in her postcode. The website brought up a list of the nearest pharmacies. 'Right. I'll be back in a minute.'

She scowled. 'You're *so* overreacting.'

No, he wasn't, he thought as he banged the door closed behind him.

If she was pregnant... Oh, hell. He'd always sworn he'd never have children, never subject another living being to the kind of childhood he'd had. But how could he possibly walk out on his child? He didn't want to be like his father had been, feckless and absent. Rico wanted his child to grow up feeling secure, knowing that both parents always would be there for him or her. A home and a life with the kind of structure and security he hadn't had until his grandparents had stepped in.

On the other hand, he didn't want to make his parents' mistakes and get married for the baby's sake. And, given how Ella's engagement had ended, he knew she wasn't going to be particularly warm to the idea of marriage, either. Though she'd admitted that she'd missed having a father, growing up.

Would she want to make a go of it with him? Though, if she did, he didn't have a clue where to start. How to be a father. How to be part of a loving family. It was completely outside his terms of reference.

What a *mess*.

Maybe she was right, and he was overreacting. But his gut told him that this was trouble.

He found the pharmacy, bought a pregnancy test kit, and went straight back to Ella. The second he walked through the door, she looked as if she was spoiling for a fight. Which wasn't what he wanted, at all. He just needed to know the truth. To know where they stood.

He handed her the packet. 'I need to know for sure, Ella. One way or the other. Please.'

That last word seemed to take the wind out of her sails, and her shoulders dropped. 'OK. I'll just be a minute.'

Though she seemed to take for ever. Why did women take so damned long to go to the loo? Rico wondered, trying to stem his frustration.

She came out holding the test stick. 'We're meant to keep it flat,' she said.

'OK. How long does it take before we get the result?'

'Two minutes—I read the instructions before I did the test.'

Oh. So that was why she'd been such a long time.

Both of them stared at the stick.

'There's a blue line in that window,' Rico said, pointing to it.

'That's the control window. It shows the test is working.'

She sounded calm, but he noticed she was gripping the stick so hard that her fingers had turned white.

A second blue line started to appear. And then it turned into a plus sign.

Positive.

She stared at him, looking utterly shocked.

Rico could barely breathe. This couldn't be happening. It really couldn't. 'One of the lines is fainter than the other.'

'It doesn't matter—if there's a plus sign, it's positive,' she said. She shook her head, as if trying to clear it.

'Pregnant. I…I can't be. I just can't.' Her face was filled with panic. 'I've just got my business off the ground. It's absolutely the wrong time for me to be pregnant. How am I going to be able to carry on the business, when I'm looking after a baby?'

He felt sick. 'So you want a termination?'

'I need to think about this.' She put her head in her hands. 'A termination would solve all the problems,' she muttered.

True. Though, if his parents had taken that route, he wouldn't be here now. And Ella wouldn't have the same dilemma in front of her. But he hated the thought of a termination. They'd just made a new life together. OK, so it hadn't been planned. But snuffing it out, as if it wasn't important… All his instincts told him that no, it wasn't what he wanted. Not at all.

Though he didn't have the right to put pressure on her. And he needed to know how she felt about this.

'Uh-huh.' He was careful to keep his voice neutral.

She looked up again, her expression tortured. 'I can't get rid of a child just because it's not convenient for me.' She dragged in a breath. 'I wasn't planned, but my mum never gave up on me, and I'm not giving up on this baby, either.' She lifted her chin. 'I promised my mum on her deathbed that I wouldn't make the same mistakes that she'd made. She never made me feel as if I was a mistake.'

Rico flinched. That definitely wasn't true for him. He'd been planned—but only by one of his parents, and not because she'd wanted him for himself. And both his parents had made him feel as if he was a mistake. A nuisance, one they only put up with so they could get the lifestyle they wanted.

'So you want to keep the baby.'

'Yes.' Her eyes were very clear. 'Which doesn't mean I'm expecting anything from you. Financial or otherwise.'

'It's my baby, too.' And, the way he saw it, there was only one way to give their baby stability and love. A traditional Italian family background. And he'd make damned sure he made a better job of it than either of their fathers had done. 'We're getting married.'

'What?' She stared at him in seeming disbelief.

'We're getting married.'

'Because of the baby?'

He rolled his eyes. 'What do you think?'

'What century are you living in?' she asked. 'People don't get married nowadays just because they're having a baby.'

'We're getting married,' he repeated.

'We are *not*.' She put her hands on her hips and glared at him. 'You told me you didn't want a family.'

'That was before you were pregnant. I'm doing the right thing by you.'

She laughed, but there was no mirth in the sound. 'Listen to yourself—do you have any idea how pompous you sound?'

'The baby is having my name.'

She rolled her eyes. 'Obviously I'll name you as the father on the birth certificate. But that's as far as it goes. You don't want a family, Rico. You don't want to get married. And I'm sure as hell not going to trap you like that and make you resent me for it later.'

The way his mother had trapped his father. She had a point. But Rico wasn't his father and Ella wasn't his mother. Surely they didn't have to repeat those mistakes?

The only way she was going to understand was if he told her about his past, the way she'd opened up to him. Trusted her. Asked her to help him change their future.

She took advantage of his silence to state her terms. 'I expect absolutely nothing from you, Rico. It's up to you how much time you want to spend with our child but, make no mistake, our child will be living with me.'

'Our child will be living with *both* of us. And we're getting married,' he repeated.

'My mother brought me up as a single mother. I've turned out perfectly fine. Our baby will be fine, too.'

She might be fine, but he definitely wasn't. 'Ella, I don't want our baby to grow up the way I did. My parents...'

There was no way out. He was going to have to tell her. Every last dragging bit of it. Even though his throat felt clogged with the words. 'My mother got pregnant with me at eighteen. On purpose. So my father would have to marry her.'

She stared at him. 'Are you saying you think I got pregnant on purpose?'

'No, of course I'm not. We're both sensible and our baby's a surprise to both of us. And you're very far from being manipulative and selfish. You're nothing like my mother.' He raked a hand through his hair. 'Ella, I don't find this easy to talk about. At all. And the only reason I'm telling you now is because it's the only way to make you understand.'

'Understand what?' She looked completely baffled.

He blew out a breath. 'I'm going to have to trust you to keep this to yourself.'

Hurt flickered on her face. 'When have I ever given you any reason not to trust me?'

'Never. I know. That came out wrong.' There was a horrible, salty taste in his mouth. 'I'm...it's...' He shook his head in frustration. Why was it so damned hard to say it? 'Hell, I've always been articulate. And yet this...it makes me feel as if my mouth's full of glue and the words can't come out.' He took a deep breath. 'I don't see my parents, Ella. I have nothing to do with them, other than giving them an allowance.'

'You give your parents an allowance?' She looked utterly shocked at the idea.

'We have a deal. They get the money to fund whatever the thrill of the month is, and they stay away from me. It suits us all perfectly.'

'Rico, I…' Her eyes were full of bewilderment. 'Why don't you want your parents anywhere near you?'

'Because they're not nice people, Ella. I'm better off without them. They never wanted me in the first place.' He couldn't look at her. Couldn't bear to see the pity in her eyes. But he owed it to her to tell the truth. 'Living with them was a nightmare. My mother got pregnant deliberately so my father would have to marry her, and she'd have the lifestyle she wanted. But they were both way too young to settle down. And they weren't suited. At all. All they did was yell at each other.'

Even now his skin felt clammy with the memory of it. 'Every day they had a fight, usually over something completely trivial. And I hated living like that. I hated all the shouting and the smashing things and the slamming doors. I went into myself, barely spoke or communicated with anyone. My teachers told my parents that I might need to go to a special school.' He dragged in a breath. 'It wasn't that I had developmental problems. I just couldn't cope with what was going on around me at home, so I closed off from everyone.'

'Oh, Rico.' She put her arms round him and held him close, as if protecting him. 'You don't have to tell me any more.'

'Yes, I do. So you can understand why I want our child to have a secure, stable home. My parents split up several times when I was little. Sometimes my mother took me with her, just to spite my father, but most of the time she forgot about me.' He dragged in a breath. 'They split up for good when I was four, nearly five. And then there was this battle for me. Not because they wanted *me*—they wanted what I represented.'

She said nothing, but she stroked his hair back from his forehead. As if she was trying to soothe him, take the pain away.

Nothing was going to take that pain away.

'For my father, I was his heir.' He smiled grimly. 'Not that Nonno was stupid enough to hand over the reins of the company to him. My father spent nearly as much money as my mother did. Fast cars, which he crashed. Boats he never even used before he sold on, at a loss. He had a real nose for investments—ones that failed, that is. But I was his bargaining chip for the future. As long as he had me, Nonno would always bail him out. Which made me a gold-mine. I wasn't his son—I was the means to an end.'

'What about your mother? I mean—she carried you for nine months. She must've adored you when you were born.'

How could Ella be that naïve, that trusting? Or maybe that was what came from knowing you were loved for yourself. Something Rico had never, ever had. 'No. For her, I was a way to get at my father. Keeping me meant that he didn't have me, and that made her feel she'd won the fight. Not to mention the extra allowance that came with me to support her lifestyle.' He sighed. 'I lived with her for a while after they split up for good. Not that I saw much of her. She slept in late every day because she was out partying every night. I had a series of indifferent nannies who brought their boyfriends round and stuck me in front of the television in the afternoons while they were...'

He coughed. 'Let's just say they were otherwise engaged behind a locked door.'

'That's awful.' Her arms tightened round him.

'And then, when my mother finally got full custody of me because the courts agreed my father was too feckless to look after me, she planned to send me to boarding school, so I'd be out of her way. She told her friends all about it when I was playing quietly in the corner of the room. I have no idea if she knew that I could hear every single word she was saying, and even if she did I don't think she cared.' He looked at Ella. 'I had everything money could buy. Every toy—all I had to do was mention it, and it would be there in every colour and size the manufacturer made. My parents tried to outdo each other in who could give me the biggest presents.'

'But you didn't have someone there for *you*. Your childhood was the total opposite of mine,' she said softly. 'My mum couldn't afford to buy me much for my birthday or Christmas. My clothes were all second-hand. But she was always there for me. She read me stories every night—from library books, because she couldn't afford to buy them. And I always, always, knew how much she loved me. She told me every single day.' She stroked his face. 'I was the lucky one, Rico. That's the kind of upbringing I want for my child. Money doesn't matter. It's how you are with people that matters.'

He knew that was true. And it turned his blood to ice. He had intentions—the very best intentions—but how would he know how to be a parent? He'd had very little to do with children. He was godfather to his best friend's children, but it was a nominal title. He was as bad as his grandparents, giving plenty in the material sense but no emotional support. He'd merely made an educated guess that his goddaughter's favourite colour was pink and his godson liked toy cars. That, or he asked Sofia, their mother, what they wanted for birthdays and Christmas.

'So did you end up at boarding school?'

'No. In the end, my grandparents took my mother to court and got custody of me.'

'So they loved you enough to rescue you.'

'To rescue the heir to the business,' he corrected. 'They sent me to various medical experts to sort me out and eventually I started talking again.' Though Rico had a feeling that that'd had less to do with the doctors and more to do with the fact that his grandparents didn't shout at each other or throw things. That he'd felt *safe* with them.

'And then, once I was reading and writing and starting to catch up with the rest of my class, my grandfather started pushing me to achieve more at school. I started work in the family business when I was fourteen. And he made it clear he expected me to do well in everything. If I wasn't top of the class, he wanted to know why. If I dropped marks in an exam, he expected me to go through it all again and work out where I'd failed and why, so I got it right next time. And if I made a mistake with the accounts or the business projections, he'd drill me in how to read a balance sheet until my head ached.'

'Did he ever say "well done"?' she asked softly.

Rico shrugged. 'He made me CEO three years ago, when he stepped down as head of the business. I guess that's the same thing. He trusts me not to mess it up. I have the final say in what happens.'

'Maybe he isn't good with words. Some people aren't good at saying what they feel.' She stroked his hair. 'What you said about your dad… He was an only child, yes?' At Rico's nod, she continued, 'Maybe your grandparents couldn't have any more children after him, so they spoiled him, poured all their love into him and gave him everything he wanted. The way he turned out, your grandparents knew they'd got it wrong. They didn't want to make those same mistakes with you, and that was why your grandfather was so hard on you when you were growing up. Like being the opposite of the way they'd been with your father, so you'd turn out OK.'

Rico had pretty much come to that conclusion himself. Though he'd rather die than actually ask his grandparents if they loved him. 'I don't want my child to grow up like that. I want to be there for my child—to be the kind of father...' He couldn't say it. He just hoped she'd realise what he meant. The kind of father he wished he'd had.

'But you're asking me to marry you for completely the wrong reason. Surely even in this day and age people get married because they love each other?'

He blew out a breath. 'That's the one thing I was hoping you weren't going to ask of me.' Because he wasn't sure he was capable of doing it. He didn't have a clue what a normal family was like. He didn't know how to love, the way she wanted him to love her. And it scared him to hell that he'd be a failure at it.

He looked absolutely terrified. And suddenly a lot of things were clear to Ella. Rico, who was calm and efficient and terribly good at business, was completely at sea when it came to emotional things. From the way he'd grown up, he didn't know how to give his heart, and he was always going to hold back from her.

Unless she could teach him to love. Give him the security he'd never had as a child. Make him realise that she valued him for himself, not for what he could give her or do for her.

If she married him, their baby would have the security she hadn't always had as a child. Two parents. What she'd always wanted, when she was younger and before she found out what a louse her father had been.

It wasn't about the money. At all. But, if she didn't marry Rico, she knew she'd struggle to cope with the business. She'd have to give it up, just when she'd got it off the ground and was doing well—that, or find a business partner to share the workload and give her time to spend with her baby, because she had no intention of neglecting her baby in favour of her career. But how could she possibly trust her judgement to find the right business partner when she was all over the place, emotionally and hormonally?

'I need to think about this,' she said. 'And right now I want to be on my own.'

For a second, she thought he flinched—as if she'd pushed him away. Given how much she knew he'd been pushed away by people in his past, it made her feel guilty. 'A lot of the time, Michael talked me round to his way of thinking, and I let him,' she said softly. 'I don't want that happening with us. Not with something this important. I just need a little time to work things out in my head—and to be sure I know what I want. And then we can talk about it, work it out between us.'

'Fair enough.' He'd switched back into efficient businessman mode and shut himself off again. She could see it in his eyes, hear it in his voice. 'Even if you decide not to marry me, Ella, you'll have my support. And I know you said it wasn't about the money, but I also know you had it hard growing up, and I'll make sure you don't ever have to worry about finances again—you or the baby. Call me when you're ready to talk.'

And he walked out without another word.

Part of Ella wanted to run after him, to tell him that she loved him and they'd work it out together. But part of her wasn't sure they could. Not if he was going to keep hold-

ing back from her. The way he could switch off like that…
she really didn't understand how he could do that. How he
could compartmentalise things so easily. Or maybe that
was his defence mechanism, and together they could learn
how to break it. Give him the chance to love her and their
baby, make a real family together.

She surveyed the kitchen. She had plenty to do. But
work could wait. Right now, she really needed to be somewhere else. She needed to think about what was happening. What Rico had offered her. If it was enough.

An hour later, she was sitting in the cemetery, putting
flowers in the vase in front of her mother's headstone.

'I wish you were here,' she said. 'You would've been
such a fabulous grandmother. Full of stories and love and
laught—' Her voice cracked halfway through the word.
'Oh, Mum. I don't know what to do. If Rico asked me to
marry him because he loved me, I'd say yes like a shot.
But it isn't why he asked me. It's so his child won't grow
up like he did. He wants to make our baby feel safe, secure, nurtured. But that isn't the same, is it?' She dragged
in a breath. 'I promised you I wouldn't make the same mistakes you did. But here I am, with an unplanned baby.' She
sniffed. 'I know you wouldn't have been like your mum
and told me to get rid of it. Rico doesn't want me to get rid
of the baby, either. I'm not under the same kind of pressure
you were. He's not like my father or Michael. He's not a
cheat. And he'd never be unfaithful to me. I guess that's
one mistake I wouldn't be repeating.'

But? She could almost hear her mother's voice asking
the question.

'But I don't know how he feels about me,' she whispered. 'I don't know if he knows how to love. Nobody's
ever really been there for him or loved him for himself.
And I think he's scared of loving me or the baby.'

She bit her lip. 'I don't want to do this on my own. You did a brilliant job with me, Mum, but I'm not you. I need someone to share this with. Someone to share the baby's first smile, the first tooth, the first word, the first step. Someone to share the tough times, to hold me when I'm panicking and tell me everything will work out just fine because we're a team.' She dragged in a breath. 'I need more support than you had. Ju would help, but it's not fair to burden her; and now I've found what I really want to do with my life, I don't want to go back to being an accountant. I know I'm being greedy, but I want it all. I want this baby, I want my career, and I want…' Her voice cracked again. 'I want Rico. I love him, Mum. He's a good man. Just a little bit lost, I think. And maybe—maybe if I let him close to me and the baby, it'll teach him to let us close to him, too. To make him realise it's safe to love us.' She bit her lip. 'And let me know it's safe to love him, too.'

Ella walked home the long way. Thinking, all the time. Could she marry Rico, knowing that he didn't love her and might never be able to love her? Could she take the risk that he'd change when the baby arrived, that he would at least fall in love with their child?

She didn't think he'd fight her for custody of the baby. Not when he'd been stuck in the middle of a custody battle himself, as a child. But what was the alternative? That he'd simply be a source of financial support? That felt wrong, too.

The more she thought about it, the more she was sure that this was the only chance Rico would ever give anyone to get really close to him. For both their sakes—and their baby's—she had to try.

When she got in, she picked up the phone.

He answered immediately. 'Rico Rossi.'

'It's Ella. I'll marry you. But I want you to know it's not about the money. It's about *sharing*.'

'Uh-huh.'

She really should've gone to see him instead of calling him. She couldn't tell a thing from that cool, neutral voice on the other end of the phone—and she needed to know how he *felt*.

Asking him would be pointless. She knew he'd stonewall her. He'd told her so much already this afternoon; no doubt right now he felt vulnerable, and he'd go into panic mode, shutting off his emotions.

Well, she felt vulnerable, too. And shutting off wasn't on her agenda.

'That means I want you to go to the scans with me. And the first ante-natal appointment.'

'Of course. I said I'd support you, Ella.'

'And,' she said, 'since we're getting married, we might as well move in together now and get used to each other, first.'

'Fine. I'll sort out an apartment here.'

'At the hotel? You're in Belgravia, Rico. Half an hour away from here. That means I'll have to get up at five in the morning to commute back here in time to start baking.'

'You don't have to commute. You can use the hotel kitchen for your work.'

No. But the only way he'd accept her refusal would be if she put it in business terms. 'That's going to make everything much more complicated. How am I going to work out my costings and my accounts, when I don't have the fuel bills to back them up? What if I get an emergency commission and I can't do it because your chefs are already using the ovens to cook for the hotel guests? I can't interrupt your business for mine.'

'I'm sure we can sort something out.'

He really was missing the point. 'I've been here before, Rico. I let someone talk me round and make decisions for me. And it all went wrong. I don't want to let that happen again, especially with a baby to consider. I want to stay *here*.'

'I'm not Michael.'

'I know.'

'And I'm not your father—or mine. I'm not going to let this fail, Ella.'

'It sounds as if you're talking about a business, Rico, not a relationship.'

He sighed. 'Business is my term of reference, Ella. It's what I'm good at.'

What about love? Though she dared not ask that. 'Rico, you do realise that this whole thing scares me as much as it scares you?'

'I'm not scared.'

She coughed. 'You promised me that you'd never lie to me again.'

He sighed. 'I know. And I told you more this afternoon than I've ever told anyone. I'm all out of words. This is the best I can offer right now, Ella.'

What choice did she have? She already knew she was in too deep. That walking away from him now would break her heart. The only thing she could do was to try with him. To teach him how to give the love that nobody had ever given him.

He'd try his best. She knew that—he'd already told her he didn't intend to be the kind of father either of them had had. But was his heart too damaged to let him be who they both wanted him to be?

'So you'll move in with me—see how it goes?'

'Do I have a choice?'

'Sure you do. You can stay in your ivory tower.'

That made him laugh. 'Ella. This isn't going to be easy for either of us. I'm not used to sharing my space. And I'm really not used to living in a broom cupboard.'

'Don't you think you can slum it for a bit, rich boy?'

'I'm definitely not answering that.' To her relief, there was a flicker of amusement in his voice. 'I'll see you later, *bellezza*. And I'll bring my suitcase.'

'Thank you.' She managed to wait until she'd put the phone down before she started crying.

Rico was going to try it her way.

And she hoped to hell they were doing the right thing.

CHAPTER THIRTEEN

TRUE to his word, Rico moved into Ella's flat that evening, and he was the one to commute to work in the mornings. He didn't make a single complaint about how small her flat was or suggest again that they should move back to The Fountain. Ella wasn't sure whether to be more relieved or surprised that he'd capitulated so easily. Did this mean that he was going to give them a real chance?

And it felt odd to be sharing her home again. To wake in the night to find a male body curled round hers. To have his razor jostling on the bathroom shelf with her hand scrub, his toothbrush next to hers in the mug, his suits next to hers in the wardrobe.

If they could make this work, then maybe her world would all come right again.

If they couldn't…

No. That wasn't an option. Somehow, she had to break through his barriers so they could make this work between them. Somehow, she needed to teach him that it was safe to love. And then it would be safe for her to love him, too.

But over the next couple of weeks she noticed that, despite their physical closeness, Rico was putting more emotional barriers up between them. Was she simply being paranoid, or was there a trapped look in his eyes? She didn't have a clue what was going on in his head, but she was pretty sure it had to do with what he'd told her about his childhood. Telling her had clearly made him feel vulnerable, and he was guarding himself again.

Didn't he know by now that he could trust her? That she'd never, ever hurt him? That she wasn't like his mother or the girlfriends in his past?

He bought her flowers. He always asked her about her day. He checked that she wasn't too tired or feeling sick. He was the perfect, solicitous partner. But if she asked him anything more personal, he'd make a vague comment and switch the conversation away from himself. And his stock response to everything was, 'I'm fine.' Even when she was damned sure he wasn't.

Still she tried to get through to him. 'How was your day?' she asked.

'Fine. I need to go back to Rome,' he said.

She froze. Did he mean for always, or just to sort out some business? He'd once told her that Rome was the only place he ever wanted to live. And she hadn't thought about whether he'd expect to move back to Rome once the baby was born, or even before that when he'd finished his business in London. 'Right,' she said carefully.

'I'll be away for three or four days.'

Not for always, then. Relief flooded through her. 'OK,' she said. Was he going to ask her to go with him?

'Will you be all right on your own while I'm away?' he asked.

That answered her question. He obviously didn't want her with him. She tried to shrug the hurt aside. 'Sure. I'm a big girl. I can look after myself,' she said brightly.

But she wondered. Would absence make Rico's heart grow fonder, or would it give him the space and time to realise that he was never going to be able to do this?

* * *

Home.

He was *home*.

Rico knew he was supposed to be feeling glad to be back in Rome, but instead he felt as if he were a stranger. He didn't really belong in the city any more. Plus that weird feeling of something being missing in his life, the one he hadn't been able to shake after Ella left but he hadn't felt since he'd been in London—that was back, big time.

And he knew why.

Because Ella wasn't here with him.

Which was ridiculous. He was going to be away on business for three or four days. Hardly any time at all. Why on earth was he missing her so badly? And so soon?

He tried dealing with it the way he always dealt with things—by blocking it out with work. Except it failed. Everywhere he looked, he saw families. Babies. Women carrying a newborn in a sling, men giving toddlers a ride on their shoulders. New parents sharing the joy of their children.

The thought slid insidiously through his head, tempting him. That was what life could be like with Ella and their baby. It didn't have to be the way his childhood had been. He just had to be brave enough to trust her with himself. To tell her that he loved her, and he was so scared that he was going to get it wrong and mess it up because he didn't have a clue how to love.

He wanted it. He wanted it so damned badly.

But he couldn't find the right words to tell her.

The first day he was away, Rico sent Ella flowers. Gorgeous summery flowers, sweet-smelling stocks and exuberant daisies and beautiful blush-pink roses. She didn't want to disturb him while he was in a meeting, so instead she took a photograph of the flowers on her phone and sent it to him with the message, *Thank you, they're gorgeous*.

His reply, a couple of hours later, was short and to the point. *Prego*.

You're welcome. That didn't bode well, she thought with a sigh. Or maybe she was reading too much into it. He was busy. At least he'd taken the time to acknowledge her text.

Though she noticed that he was too busy to call her even for two minutes.

OK. She could deal with this. As she'd said to him, she was an adult and she could look after herself.

The second day, he sent her chocolates. And a seriously nasty thought hit her. Was Rico choosing the gifts, or had he delegated the task to his secretary? Particularly as his only contact with her was a brief text message in reply to her thanks for the chocolates, saying he hoped she was OK.

On the third day, there was a delivery of a blu-ray disc of a film she'd mentioned casually that she'd like to see. She smiled wryly. She didn't actually have a blu-ray player, though she didn't quite have the heart to tell him that his gift had misfired. He'd listened enough to get the film right; it wasn't his fault that she hadn't upgraded the format. Although she really, really wanted to hear his voice, Rico had made it pretty clear that he was communicating by text only while he was away, so she tried not to mind and sent him a text to thank him.

'How did you know Sofia was the right one for you?' Rico asked his best friend, turning his wine glass round in his hands. He couldn't look Giuseppe in the eye. They never talked about this sort of thing, about emotions and love

and family. But Rico really needed to know, and his best
friend was about the only person he could ask. *How* did
you know someone was the right one for you?

'Because life without her was unthinkable,' Giuseppe
replied simply.

Yeah. That worked for him, too. Life without Ella...
He'd been without her for three days and he was a total
mess. He couldn't wait to get back to London. Back to *her*.

'Why are you asking? Is this the woman you borrowed
the plane for?'

This time, Rico met his gaze head on. 'Yes.'

'It's serious, then.' Giuseppe raised an eyebrow. 'I never
thought I'd see the day. Are you OK?'

'Yes.' But Giuseppe had known him for years. And he
was the only person Rico had let close to him. The only
one Rico trusted, or he would never have started this conversation in the first place. 'No.' He sighed. 'I hate this,
Seppe. I don't feel in control any more.'

'Sounds about right,' Giuseppe said. 'If it helps, it does
get better.'

'Does it?' Rico wasn't so sure. 'And what if I get it
wrong?'

'Then you learn to apologise. Flowers and chocolates
usually work.'

Rico smiled wryly. 'I've already sent them.'

'And the words?' Giuseppe asked. 'Because that's what
Sofia expects more than anything. The words.'

'What words?' Sofia asked, coming in and leaning on
her husband's shoulder.

Giuseppe stretched up to kiss her. *'Ti voglio molto
bene.'*

She smiled. 'I love you very much too, Seppe.' She
looked at Rico. 'I only caught the last few words, but

does this mean you've finally stopped dating those awful women and you've found yourself someone nice?'

That wasn't the half of it. He decided to cut to the chase. 'How do you two feel about being godparents?'

Sofia's jaw dropped. 'You're kidding! You…baby… You…'

He'd never seen his best friend's wife lost for words before. Sofia could talk the hind leg off a donkey. Rico grinned. 'Yes. I'm going to be a dad.' It was the first time he'd said the words out loud. And something cracked inside him; his skin felt too tight. As if he were going to burst with love and pride.

Ella was having their baby. And the world, which had seemed so messed-up the last few weeks, tilted and righted itself. Except everything was different. Like walking from a monochrome into full, vibrant colour. Because the woman he loved was giving him the most precious gift in the world. And now he knew what to tell her.

'I was intending just to offer to get you two some more wine and leave you both to another boring conversation about cars,' Sofia said, 'but not now.' She took a glass from the cupboard and topped up their glasses as well as filling her own. 'I want to know *everything.*'

'Uh.' Panicked, Rico looked to Giuseppe to rescue him.

Giuseppe simply spread his hands. 'You heard the lady.' He smiled. 'I want to know, too. But I do know one thing. She has to be special.'

Rico frowned. 'Why?'

'To make you fall in love with her. Because you always keep people at a distance—even us, to some extent,' Giuseppe said gently.

'Yes, she's special. And yes, I love her.' Actually saying

the words made him feel a whole lot better. Rico smiled. 'OK. You want to know about my Ella *bellezza*. I'll tell you.'

Later that evening, when the horn beeping outside signalled the arrival of Rico's taxi, Sofia hugged him. 'Stay happy,' she said. 'And next time you come to Rome, bring Ella with you.'

'Or you could come to London to meet her. I know a nice little hotel where you could stay,' he said with a smile. 'And bring the children. I know some places they'll love.'

Giuseppe patted his shoulder. 'I never thought I'd hear something like *that* from you. But it's good. You've finally put the past where it belongs. And, for what it's worth, I think you're going to be a great dad.'

'Not perfect,' Rico said. He knew he was very far from perfect.

'Nobody's perfect,' Sofia said gently. 'Just do your best. That'll be good enough.'

Rico only hoped that she was right.

Back at the hotel, he glanced at his watch. Even allowing for the time difference, it was late. And pregnancy had made Ella sleepy. It wouldn't be fair to ring her and wake her up, just to tell her that he loved her. He didn't want to say it in a text, either. These were words he needed to tell her out loud. In the end, he just sent her a text. *Back tomorrow.*

And in the morning he'd make time to go shopping. For something he should've bought her weeks ago.

This was the fourth day without a single word. Rico hadn't even sent her a text today.

Ella had to face it. He wasn't ever going to be able to

love her. Sure, he'd sent her gifts—thoughtful gifts—but that wasn't what she wanted. She wanted his heart, and he'd never be able to give it to her.

Which meant their marriage was going to be loveless.

Promise me you won't make the same mistakes I did, Ella.

Falling for a man who couldn't love her back? A good man, but nevertheless that was exactly what she'd done. So very, very stupid.

No way could she marry him. And, even though she knew he was probably busy, in a meeting or something, she needed to tell him.

But when she called, his phone went straight through to voicemail.

She knew she should leave it until she spoke to him in person. Doing this by voicemail was utterly selfish. But she also knew she was weak, where he was concerned. If she left it until she saw him, she might not have the courage to tell him how she felt. And that wasn't fair on either of them. 'Rico, it's Ella. I'm sorry. I can't do this. Obviously you'll have access to the baby, if you want it—we'll sort that out so it's fair for all of us—but I'm sorry, I can't marry you.'

When she hung up, she drew her knees up to her chin and wrapped her arms round her legs. Though she couldn't cry. Sometimes pain went way too deep for tears.

Rico was glad he'd brought next to nothing back to London with him. Just one piece of hand luggage and his laptop case. He would've gone crazy if he'd had to wait at baggage reclaim.

Customs seemed to take for ever.

But finally he was through. He switched his phone on, intending to ring Ella and tell her he'd be home in less than an hour, when his phone beeped to let him know there was a voicemail.

Well, it could wait. Ella was more important.

But her mobile phone was switched off, and there was no answer from her landline. That meant she was either up to her eyes in the kitchen, or she was out on a delivery and had forgotten to switch her mobile on. She'd become incredibly scatty over the last couple of weeks and had to leave herself sticky notes all over the place.

Smiling at the thought, he listened to the voicemail. And his blood went cold.

I can't marry you.

What?

Why?

He tried her mobile again, and her landline, still with no result.

Oh, hell. He needed to see her, find out what was going on. Why couldn't she marry him? A seriously nasty thought struck him. Had she met someone else? No. Ella wasn't like that. Though she'd said that her ex had talked her round before. Had he talked her round again? Was Ella still in love with him?

He drove too fast on the way back to London, and only a near miss when someone pulled out in front of him made him slow down. It felt like for ever until his key was unlocking the front door, and he took the stairs up to the flat two at a time.

She wasn't there.

And her mobile phone was *still* switched off.

He paced the flat. Made himself coffee. Paced the flat. Tried her phone again. Paced the flat. And he was a hair's-breadth away from going insane when he heard the front door being unlocked.

Thank God. She was home. And they could sort this mess out.

She looked wary when she saw him. 'Rico. I didn't know when you were going to be back.'

'I should've told you. I'm sorry.'

She swallowed hard. 'Did you...did you get my message?'

'Yes.' And it hurt like hell. 'Why can't you marry me, Ella?'

'Because I've had time to think while you were away. You didn't call me—and I don't think you're ever going to be able to love me. I can't handle a loveless marriage.' Tears shimmered in her eyes. 'I'm sorry. I won't ever fight you, the way your mum fought your dad. I want you to be as much a part of the baby's life as you want to be. But I can't do this any more. I can't pretend everything's OK. And I'm not going to make the same mistake my mum made, falling for someone who's never going to love me back.'

Never going to love me back.

Those words gave him the courage that her voicemail had leached away. She loved him. Right now, she didn't believe in him, but that was his own fault for holding back. And he could do something about that.

'You're not making your mother's mistake,' he said. 'You *haven't* fallen for someone who doesn't love you back. You've fallen for someone who's totally rubbish at emotions and who isn't very good at telling you how he feels. But I'm going to try to change that, Ella. I'll need your help, but I swear to you I'm going to try my hardest.'

She stared at him as if he were speaking Martian.

He frowned. 'I'm speaking English, yes? Not rambling on in Italian?'

That made her smile. 'You never ramble, Rico.'

'Maybe I should learn.' He couldn't stand being apart from her any more. He closed the space between them and wrapped his arms round her. 'I'm going to need help with this. I've never told anyone I loved them before. Opening myself up like this—it feels weird. Scary. As if I'm standing on the edge of a precipice and someone's about to shove me over. But I love you, Ella. I really do.' He pulled away so he could look her in the eye. 'It scares me to death. I'm so scared of failing you. But I love you.'

'Really?' Her eyes were full of tears.

'I love you and I want to be with you. And our baby.' He rested his hand protectively on her abdomen. 'I don't exactly have good role models when it comes to parenting. Except Sofia and Seppe—and Sofia tells me that nobody's perfect and my best will be good enough.'

'Sofia?'

Was it his imagination, or did she sound just the tiniest bit jealous? 'My best friend's wife. And I have a confession to make.' He dragged in a breath. 'I, um, asked them to be godparents, just as I'm godfather to their children. Except they'll be better at it than I am. Do you mind?'

She blinked. 'You told them about me? And the baby?'

'Everything. They already know you're special.' He smiled. 'Seppe says for me to let anyone close, she has to be seriously special. And you are.'

She swallowed hard. 'You really love me?'

'I've been trying to tell myself I didn't. When I looked you up in London, it was to prove to myself that what we had was just sex.'

'Acquaintances with benefits.'

He grimaced. 'You're so much more than that to me. I was in denial even then. The very fact I had to prove to myself that you weren't special—well, it was because deep down I knew you *were*.' He blew out a breath. 'And

Rome—Rome isn't home to me any more. I hated being there without you.'

'Why didn't you ask me to go with you?'

'Because I didn't even want to admit to myself that I needed you. But I do need you, Ella.' He stroked her face. 'And I'm sorry. I should've told you that first day I was away. But I didn't know how to say it. And I didn't want to send you a text.'

'You sent me flowers.'

'The nearest I've ever got to love in the past is expensive presents. And I know that's not what love's about. I got it so badly wrong. Will you give me another chance, *bellezza*?'

A tear trickled down her cheek. 'You love me.'

'And our baby. I can't wait to be a dad. And I can't wait to marry you. I know you said you couldn't marry me, but that was when you thought I didn't love you. Now you know I do…will you change your mind?'

Ella could hardly believe what she was hearing. Was she dreaming? Imagining the words she'd so longed to hear from him?

'I went shopping this morning. For something important. I know you've been here before—but I'm not Michael. I'm not going to cheat on you. I'm not going to lie to you. And I might need reminding to open up to you, but I'm going to try my hardest to make you happy. To make you know how very, very much I love you.' He dropped down on one knee in front of her and drew a box from his pocket; he opened it to reveal a very simple band of diamonds in what looked to her like platinum.

She gasped. 'It's like the Sisi star you bought me, all sparkly—it's beautiful.'

'I'm glad you like it, because I need to ask you something. Last time, I got it wrong. I demanded. This time, I'm going to do it properly. I want to do it right.' He took her hand. 'Will you marry me, Ella? And I need you to know that I don't want to marry you just because of the baby. I want to marry you because of *you*. Because my life's a lot better with you in it. And you make me whole.'

She felt the tears gather in her eyes. 'Oh, Rico.'

'And I want to make sure that our baby knows from their very first breath that they're loved for who they are. Just as I love you for who you are, and you love me the same way—at least, I hope you do.' His breath caught. 'And I'm not good at this stuff, so I'm going to need your help in getting it right. I need you, Ella. I love you.'

She blinked the tears back. 'I love you, too. I love you for who you are. I don't give a damn about your money or your status or any of that rubbish. It's you I love. If you lost everything tomorrow, and my business went under, we'd still cope.' She stroked his face. 'Yes. I'll marry you, Rico. I'll be proud to marry you. And…' She took a deep breath. 'If you really need to go back to Rome, I'll go with you.'

'I can be based anywhere. If you want to stay in London, we'll stay here. Or we can live in Rome. Vienna. Even Timbuktu!' He kissed her. 'It doesn't matter where we live, as long as we're together. You were absolutely right. It doesn't matter whether we live in a broom cupboard in London or half the top floor of a posh hotel in Rome. It's being together that matters. You've taught me that and I'll never, ever forget it.'

He meant it. She knew he meant every single word.

And she also knew that she could trust him, and he'd never let her down. 'You've taught me a lot, too. You've made me see that not all men are liars. Well, I knew they weren't, but you know what I mean. You've taught me that it's safe to rely on you, because you'll never let me down.'

He slipped the ring onto the third finger of her left

hand. 'And there's a lot we've still got to learn. But we'll get there, because we'll be learning together.'

'Together,' she echoed with a smile.

And she knew that, as long as they had each other, everything was going to work out just fine.

* * * * *

A sneaky peek at next month...

MODERN™

INTERNATIONAL AFFAIRS, SEDUCTION & PASSION GUARANTEED

My wish list for next month's titles...

In stores from 17th August 2012:

❑ Unlocking her Innocence – Lynne Graham
❑ His Reputation Precedes Him – Carole Mortimer
❑ Just One Last Night – Helen Brooks
❑ The Husband She Never Knew – Kate Hewitt

In stores from 7th September 2012:

❑ Santiago's Command – Kim Lawrence
❑ The Price of Retribution – Sara Craven
❑ The Greek's Acquisition – Chantelle Shaw
❑ When Only Diamonds Will Do – Lindsay Armstrong
❑ The Couple Behind the Headlines – Lucy King

Available at WHSmith, Tesco, Asda, Eason, Amazon and Apple

Just can't wait?

0812/01

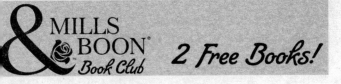

MILLS & BOON Book Club

2 Free Books!

Get your free books now at
www.millsandboon.co.uk/freebookoffer

Or fill in the form below and post it back to us

THE MILLS & BOON® BOOK CLUB™—HERE'S HOW IT WORKS: Accepting your free books places you under no obligation to buy anything. You may keep the books and return the despatch note marked 'Cancel'. If we do not hear from you, about a month later we'll send you 4 brand-new stories from the Modern™ series priced at £3.49* each. There is no extra charge for post and packaging. You may cancel at any time, otherwise we will send you 4 stories a month which you may purchase or return to us—the choice is yours. *Terms and prices subject to change without notice. Offer valid in UK only. Applicants must be 18 or over. Offer expires 31st January 2013. **For full terms and conditions, please go to www.millsandboon.co.uk/freebookoffer**

Mrs/Miss/Ms/Mr (please circle)

First Name

Surname

Address

Postcode

E-mail

Send this completed page to: Mills & Boon Book Club, Free Book Offer, FREEPOST NAT 10298, Richmond, Surrey, TW9 1BR

Find out more at
www.millsandboon.co.uk/freebookoffer

Visit us Online

0712/P2YEA